倍斯特出版事業有限公司
Best Publishing Ltd.

雅思
閱讀聖經

韋爾 ◎ 著

QRCODE
DOWNLOAD
英式發音

U0066439

《劍16》加持
破解「試題」，秒答9成試題，直取8.0

核心語法強化，內建考官邏輯腦

關鍵語法融入《劍》16精隨，掌握各種「同義改寫」、「定位點」，迅速拆解魔王級難題，跨過8分門檻。

從考「古」題中延伸「新」穎試題，大幅提升臨場應對能力

規劃「古」＋「新」合併考題，迅速活化思緒、舉一反三，任何題型變化均能觸類旁通獲取高分。

PRE FACE 作者序

在《*Getting There*》中，CBS 執行長曾提及，有時候公司年度所推出的三部劇，其中的兩部並未叫座，這也彰顯出在美劇電視圈要有數部成功的劇集並賺取金錢著實不易。美劇並不像是台劇等劇集，其每季可能僅有 10-23 集（每一集的製作成本都相當昂貴）。當中很多劇僅推出了第一季就結束了。你看到市面上有拍攝到第四季的影集已經算是相當熱門了（畢竟在每季結束後還需要有電視台或有投資客等願意續訂這部影集）。當中也有位我喜歡的明星在拍攝影集後，後來公司打算不出了，而還有另一位是劇集僅播放到第一季的前幾集，就被電視台高層要求砍掉。當然電視台會有「備案」以備不時之需，畢竟每年有那麼多的製作人等向他們推銷影集。在這樣的競爭壓力下，第一季的第一集就非常重要，一定要是高收視率才行。最後我從中找出了其中兩部在第一季都採取了類似的手法讓收視率飆高的影集。

保證高收視的其中一個原因就是「面試」（當然還必須要搭配緊湊的情節、具演技的演員等等的要素），觀眾喜歡看面試的原因不外乎是每個人在人生的任何階段，只要必須要找工作，就必須要參加面試。當中我選的兩部是《金權遊戲》和《金裝律師》，（其實電影 *The Devil Wears Prada* 也是）。兩部在第一季的呈現都很棒，礙於篇幅，我以其中的《金權遊戲》來做介紹。Ellen Parsons 是位優秀的法律系畢業生，在第一集的前段也獲得 A 律師事務所的認可並欲與她談工作的薪資和獎金，但是 Ellen Parsons 也將眼光放到像 Patty Hewes 這樣的公司。（她甚至在 A 律師事務所面談結束後，不諱言的跟其他面試官表明她還有 Patty Hewes 的公司的面談。）

看的當下我內心的疑問是，像 Patty Hewes 這樣的公司會需要 Ellen Parsons 嗎？（在 Patty Hewes 這樣經手一個法律 case 可能就能從中獲利數億到數十億美元的公司，該公司本來就有很多具有實務經驗的律師了，外加有那麼多有名校法律系畢業且具備實務經驗的律師可以挑選，如果 Patty Hewes 的公司選擇她，那麼背後應該有目的才對。）在 A 律師事務所的面談後，Ellen Parsons 前往 Patty Hewes 的公司參加面談。她遇到面試官 Tom（Tom 算是公司的合夥人兼 Patty Hewes 的朋友）他沒有使用任何的面試伎倆等等，就是一場很真誠的面談，後面或許是出於投緣等等，他還給予 Ellen Parsons 許多面試提點，告訴她在面對老闆 Patty Hewes 的面談時該注意些什麼，就這樣面試進行得很順利，直到 Tom 向 Ellen Parsons 告知下次面試的時間時，Ellen 有點驚訝萬分。面試的時間是週六，但是週六是她妹妹的婚禮，而這個面試是個千載難逢的機會，她到底該如何做出選擇？（相信看到這裡很多觀眾就會選擇繼續看下去，而不會轉台了，因為會想要知道 Ellen 到底該怎麼選擇呢？後面的劇情也很耐人尋味。）

PREFACE 作者序

　　另一部影集則是與「逆境」有關聯。在觀看很多 po 文後,又把面對逆境(哲學＋人生觀)的主題,放入了這次的目次裡(在雅思實際考試中也有與此相關聯的主題,像是 optimism 或是 negative emotion 等,而這類的主題通常不難)。其中要提的是《*Ugly Betty*》中的女主角 Wilhelmina Slater(她的角色跟電影 *The Devil Wears Prada* 中史翠普所演的時尚女魔頭一樣)。Slater 在時尚女魔頭 Fey Sommer 手下當助理,後來爬升到現在總編的位子。當中她用了許多手段和伎倆,在第三季後,我覺得她討喜許多。她後來面臨很多困境,這些問題卻一股腦的出現在她眼前。其中,她成功地獲取了跟出版商老闆兒子同樣都是總編的身分,且兩個人都各有公司 50%的股份。但是後來,公司財務長掏空了公司所有資金,雖然後來有投資客注入資金讓公司得以營運,不過她在公司的地位已經大不如前。

　　在第四季中,模特兒們在巴哈馬的拍攝就是她離職前最後一次以身兼總編的身分親自到現場視察(她離職前的最後作品)。其實她暗中也有規劃備案,以她在時尚圈的影響力和知名度,她計畫要跳到 B 公司去工作。在巴哈馬愜意的海灘上,她看到房內電視牆上,電視畫面播放著,另一個時尚界的競爭對手 C 比她搶先一步獲取了該工作。C 在接受記者採訪時與自己女兒站在一塊,看起來容光煥發,甚至還硬是說了一句 How can a girl get so lucky,似乎在反諷

Slater。（C 的家庭美滿，而且有個貌美如花的女兒，再加上她獲取了新的工作。）對比之下，Slater 連唯一支撐她走下去的工作都要失去了，新的工作也沒著落。Slater 目前沒有伴，且她沒有像 C 一樣有著支持自己事業的丈夫，雪上加霜的是她跟女兒的關係也不好（因為一直以來，她都把所有心思都放在工作上了）。絕望之餘，她無奈且落魄地走到海灘的某處，狼狽地啃著漢堡。她曾不允許編輯在公司內吃貝果等等，因為覺得很 low。但此時此刻，她似乎不在乎被其他人拍到，甚至嘲諷她「怎麼一個時尚總編在這裡失魂落魄、不修邊幅地啃著漢堡」。這無疑是她人生最低潮的時刻，問題是，這一切會有轉機嗎？

　　另外要提的是美劇《美少女的謊言》，這是一部我完全沒預期要看的劇（也一些朋友疑惑著詢問說怎麼會看這個），我之前也總會想，高中的劇應該要是浪漫的戀愛劇（但是這樣浪漫的戀愛劇儘管主角等外貌都很出眾，觀看久了真的蠻膩，甚至許多劇情和對話都能自己杜撰出）。劇中有 5 位女主角，裡面的帶頭者是 Allison，但是 Allison 在第一季第一集結尾，警方發現了她的屍體。其他四位女主角對此也感到震驚，她們都以為傳訊息給自己的 A 是 Allison。這樣的安排也讓許多觀眾思考著那麼 A 到底是誰？帶著懸疑和恐怖氣氛的劇情，也讓這部戲在眾多青少年劇中脫穎而出。（其實仔細看在第一季和第三季都有些細微的線索在，關於 A 是誰在此就不劇透了，許多觀眾更是把女主角和女主角的曖昧對象、同學和男朋友等全都猜過一遍了。）俗話說：「三個臭皮匠勝過一個諸葛亮」，而女主角還剩四位，再加上那些男友、家長和警方，鬥不過一個 A 嗎？（也因為如此讓我接著看了這部劇。）

　　關於 Allison，我只覺得沒有父母可以管得動她，她做了太多令人髮指的事情了，許多事情都玩得過頭了，甚至會耍閨蜜，並以此為樂。例如在第二季某一集，Allison 請四位女閨蜜從萬聖節派對，到一間空屋找她，四人屏氣凝神地到了空屋並找尋 Allison，最後來到一間房間裡，卻沒見到 Allison，突然間房門自己關上，緊接著就聽到 Allison 被追殺和打鬥的聲音。情急之下，四個女主角拿起手機，想打 911 求救，但是手機都沒有訊號。接著只能透過門孔觀看一個帶著舞會面具的男子跟 Allison 的打鬥畫面 ...Allison 更有可能因此在四個閨蜜注視下被殺死，最後才知道是 Allison 耍四個閨蜜的，她請人來演這齣戲。這就是 Allison。隨後 Allison 回到萬聖節派對遇到 Noel，她表達了感謝，感謝 Noel 配合她演戲嚇嚇閨蜜，但是 Noel 表明剛剛有事耽擱了，所以沒辦法過去，Allison 內心嚇得半死，那麼剛剛在空屋戴面具的男生是誰？（Allison 就是這樣常玩得過頭了。）

　　另外要提的是跟魚的構造圖有關的電影。《第六感奇緣之人魚傳說》是一部新奇、俊男美女雲集的一部電影。在生物學的課堂中，生物老師在黑板上所陳列的「魚的結構圖（英文版）」，這在雅思考試中也確實出現過。在電影中，生物老師正在講解魚的構造圖，卻目睹金城武所飾的男主角正在打瞌睡，懲罰他後，隨即要求笑得過頭的鍾麗緹所飾的小美（小美其實是條美人魚），將寫著英文敘述的提示卡正確地擺放至黑板上魚的構造圖旁。但是老師不知道小美是條美人魚，這對她來說實在是太輕而易舉了。魚的構造圖和相關部位在雅思聽力和閱讀都常出現。在聽力中鯨豚類的題材，就常會有 dorsal fin 等的訊息出現。在閱讀中如果再遇到這樣的圖表題，更能省下考生許多時間。如果有 7 題的話，考生在一分鐘內找到對應訊息並寫好答案在答案卡上。在接下來的 59 分鐘答剩餘的 33 題題目，遠比 60 分鐘答 40 題題目更為充裕。（這也說明了，掌握考古題的重要性，有剛好遇到類似或一樣的題目就等於賺到了。）

　　礙於篇幅，其他目次內的內容再請觀看書籍內容，最後要提到的是八方旅人，因為遊戲類的話題在雅思中出現，像是「Nintendo 和 Sony」，不過出題者有大幅降低出題難度。（本來要寫八方旅人的歷史部分，不過考量難度會太高，所以改成寫其他內容。）遊戲類話題也比較會是吸引男生的主題，所以有平衡掉像是美少女的謊言的選題比較吸引女生。（畢竟推出一個商品最大考量還是要能同時吸引男生和女生。像是遊戲仙劍一，就同時能吸引男生和女生玩家，且儘管後來的動畫製作等不斷地提升，但如果去問玩過仙劍的玩家，大家永遠會說最好的還是仙劍一。）

　　此外，雅思備考和八方旅人有極大的關聯性，從遊戲中也能協助考生修正備考而有更好的學習成果。八方旅人遊戲最後要打最終BOSS，經過爬文和看很多影片後，我統計出玩家平均破關的時數大概在 70-75 小時，也有玩家是玩到 110 小時平均等級 85 級才破關，甚至有玩家 28 小時就破關了。破關時間的長短，似乎等同於雅思備考，即**大家起始點都相同或裝備都相同的情況下，為什麼會有這麼大的顯著差異存在呢？**當中更有不少玩家抱怨最終 BOSS 太難打或是選擇放棄打了（也有玩家甚至花了 1 小時半才打死王），選擇直接看其他人的破關影片畫面。

　　❶有些玩家認為在某個平均等級無法打贏時，初步的想法就是，只好繼續衝等級，然後繼續試試看。但是從破關等級來看有些人平均等級 65 左右就能打贏最終 Boss，而且根據等級數值的統計，hp 和 sp 如果沒有差到 20 級其實角色能力數值沒有差到那麼大，**重點還是在角色技能的掌握和攻略王的方式**。這點可以對應到，有的考生會認為需要背到單字量 12000-15000 甚至以上才能達到某個分數段，但實際上優秀的考生就像是平均 65 等的玩家一樣，僅掌握比指考字彙稍難的字彙量就考取某個分數段。這點也能從劍橋雅思題本的

聽力和閱讀答案表中回推，並沒有過難的單字，甚至聽力都是非常基礎的生活常用字。何況還有其他核心語法等可以協助攻略字彙量不足的部分，例如某些專有名詞，專有名詞一定有類似同位語等以更簡單的方式去解釋這個詞，所以其實你不知道某個單字，你也能從一些敘述和解釋中理解並答題。（這跟平均 65 級的玩家一樣，他們一定有掌握一些關鍵和方法，但絕不是將重點放在要衝更高的等級，才能將最終 BOSS 打死）

❷有些玩家在打完某些地圖或主線的 BOSS 後信心滿滿，但是看到其他玩家的影片，卻滿腹狐疑，因為具備同等裝備的情況下，怎麼自己的攻擊數值不如其他玩家呢？關於這點，**很明顯的是在於角色各個技能和輔助技能的了解不足所造成的**。可能到遊戲破關了也還不懂。例如：每個角色的物力或魔法攻擊數值最大只有 9999，其他玩家卻能有破萬或數萬的攻擊數值。這是因為玩家忘了替該角色裝備**「突破傷害限制」**，在裝備這項輔助技能後，角色的攻擊數值就能超過 9999。這也是造成有些玩家打王的回合數總是比別人多數個回合等等的原因。關於這點又能回推到雅思備考，例如：不具備掌握跳讀等閱讀技能的學習者，始終比其他學習者在寫官方試題和考場試題時更為費力，常常覺得時間不夠用。

❸有些玩家在不懂一些技能的使用和角色能力時，已經有「先

入為主」的判斷，認為某些職業很難用。事實上，第一個主要角色選「學者」是最棒的，但每個角色和每個技能會被設計出都是有原因在的。有些玩家有抱怨「獵人」，但是獵人的捕獲獵物技能其實非常實用，例如在打最終 BOSS 時招喚嗜夢，一次攻擊就能打到 5 萬，佔王的血量的 1/10 了（打最終 BOSS 使用獵人的召喚獵物協助戰鬥的部分，我想是那些放棄打王的玩家所沒有想到可以使用的策略），而且還有很多非主線地圖的魔物對於打最終 BOSS 很有用，不能光仰賴獵人的物理攻擊去打最終 BOSS 的，可能會打到天荒地老。又或是舞孃的技能「不可思議之舞」，有一定機率讓戰鬥獲得的經驗值變 100 倍，也有外國玩家用這個很快就達到平均等級 93 級。真的有很多部分是你沒有考慮到的。

❹還有就是「反向思考」和「大膽做決定」。以雅思來說，第一次大腦所評估的判斷題的答案為何就是那個答案了，更改後反而是錯誤的，而且要很快地做出決定，因為考場中分秒必爭，在猶豫中時間就不斷地流逝掉了。反向思考的話，就如同在遊戲中，每個角色都同時損血 1-2000 的時候，你會選擇先補血還是繼續反擊。我是選擇不補血繼續打王，可能在多攻擊一兩次王就死了，戰鬥就結束了。不過有些玩家會選擇先補血，於是就越打越久。其實也關乎到另一個遊戲中的設定，例如「藥師」有死裡求生斬、「劍士」有輔助技能火場怪力，這些都代表著血量越低時，攻擊力更大，所以你更該趁勝追擊

才對。在雅思考試中也是，有些考題是需要反向思考的或是直接先跳過找不到對應訊息的題目等等，而關於遊戲和雅思的關聯性有很多，這部分再請考生觀看內文的解析和解題策略了，最後祝所有考生都考取理想成績。

韋爾 敬上

INSTRUCTIONS
使用說明

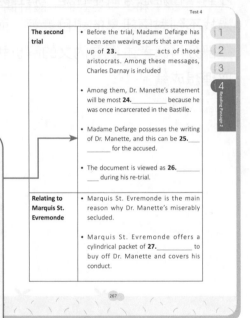

Questions 20-27
Complete the summary using the list of words and phrases A-Q below
Write the correct letter, A-Q in boxes 20-27 on your answer sheet.

A Tale of Two Cities	EVENTS
Relating to Sydney Carton	• Charles Darnay's **20.** _____ destiny is overturned by Sydney Carton's willingness to make a sacrifice, making

The second trial	• Before the trial, Madame Defarge has been seen weaving scarfs that are made up of **23.** _____ acts of those aristocrats. Among these messages, Charles Darnay is included
	• Among them, Dr. Manette's statement will be most **24.** _____ because he was once incarcerated in the Bastille.
	• Madame Defarge possesses the writing of Dr. Manette, and this can be **25.** _____ for the accused.
	• The document is viewed as **26.** _____ during his re-trial.
Relating to Marquis St. Evremonde	• Marquis St. Evremonde is the main reason why Dr. Manette's miserably secluded.
	• Marquis St. Evremonde offers a cylindrical packet of **27.** _____ to buy off Dr. Manette and covers his conduct.

納入「亂序出題」
提升試題鑑別度和考生整合答題實力
並強化「同義轉換」和「推測」能力
任何出題均能應付裕如

• 亂序出題對大多數考生造成了許多
答題上的難點,且拉長了答題時
間,尤其是考生必須要確實理解並
且釐清敘述事件後才能答對。藉由
雙城記難度較高的敘述文搭配亂序
出題,考生只要反覆演練這篇就能
掌握相關答題技能,立即獲取理想
成績。

• 題目設計中加入更隱晦的改寫表
達,且出題與官方出題完全一致,
強化考生高階同義轉換能力和突破
更高分閱讀關卡的必備綜合技能。

超強獨創三合一

「影子跟讀」和「中英對照」設計閱讀文章均錄音且納入語法強化

- 閱讀文章每篇均錄音，有效輔助仰賴耳朵聽以學習的考生。此外，考生更能同步運用音檔作影子跟讀練習，提升聽力專注力和口說能力。

- 聆聽音檔，藉由精選試題中各篇章的文句大幅強化考生 **Academic Writing** 的實力，一次就考取寫作 **7.5** 分以上的得分。

- 閱讀文章中英對照，便於基礎學習者藉由中譯輔助學習，自學就能達到理想成績。

- 迅速破解**摘要題**和**選擇式配對題**等題型，因為即使依據關鍵字定位到某句話後，能須仰賴**語法**來協助答題的題型，在更短時間內答完更具精心設計的題目或陷阱題。

B. In *Gone with the Wind*, Scarlett's father, Gerald has provided his wisdom about love to Scarlett in an earlier chapter, when he senses something is going on between Scarlett's mind. He says "Have you been running after a man who's not in love with you, when

you could have any of the bucks in the County?" and "Our people and the Wilkes are different." Still Scarlett does not know the nuances and read between the lines, and goes down the road of pursuing Ashley Wilkes. Even though she has many pursuers, Scarlett does not even know what love is. Scarlett does not have to go through the meandering route, if she knows what she wants and she knows what her father has said to her. Even Melanie knows better than she knows herself, so when there is a rumor between Scarlett and Ashley, Melanie knows Scarlett cannot have a feeling towards Ashley. If Scarlett had known herself, she wouldn't have made the statement "He never really existed at all, except in my imagination." at the very end of the fiction.

在《亂世佳人》早先的章節中，思嘉莉的父親，傑拉爾德就提供了他對思嘉莉愛情的智慧之言，當他感受到思嘉莉的心理有著不尋常的念頭時。他說「妳一直追著不愛妳的男人跑，而妳實際上卻可以擁有那裡任何一個男人？」而且「我們家族和威爾克斯家族是截然不同的」。思嘉莉仍舊察覺不出其中的細微差異並了解當中的言外之意，她繼續朝著追求艾希禮、威爾克斯之路邁進。即使她也能知道自己要什麼且了解她父親所對她說的話，那麼她就不用走那條蜿蜒蜒的路。甚至瑪蘭都比她更了解她自己，所以當思嘉莉和艾希禮之前傳

H. Between pelvic fins and caudal fins, it's anal fins. Anal fins are also called cloacal fins, which have the function of stabilizing the fish.

I. Aside from those above-mentioned functions, fins have other purposes, too. Fins can also be used as the delivery for sperm, and caudal fins have the function of stupefying the prey. That is quite a common function that we know about tail fins that are functioned as forward moment and stability. In addition, in some species, there are spines hidden in the dorsal fins that can insert venom into the prey. Pectoral fins also have distinctive functions that give the fish animated lifting to capture flying fish. The anatomy of fish is not that hard to grasp. If you were a high school student, you obviously wouldn't need the flair of Xiao Mei to impress your biology lecturer or crack IELTS reading parts.

英文試題

Questions 14-19

Label the diagram below
Choose NO MORE THAN TWO WORDS from the passage for each answer.
Write your answers in boxes 14-19 on your answer sheet.

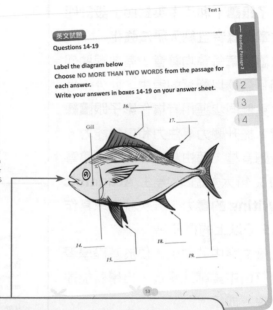

精選圖表題並結合電影

從考「古」題中延伸「新」穎試題,大幅提升臨場應對能力

【時間統籌】強化,思緒更靈巧,時間更充裕

- 規劃「古」+「新」合併考題,迅速活化思緒、舉一反三,任何題型變化均能觸類旁通獲取高分。
- 納入各種解題技巧和推測能力,迅速理解並對應到圖表中的專有名詞,省掉大幅查找的時間。
- 亦規劃了同步答此篇其他兩個題型的答題,一次攻略三種類型題目的設計,強化時間統籌能力。

破解雅思三個單項設計

聽、讀和寫同步強化

優化閱讀速度、打好聽力基礎

寫出 **7.5** 以上高分範文

三個單項的分數同步飆升

- 閱讀文章均附音檔，協助考生內建學術佳句，讀、寫同步強化，節省 60% 備考時間，一次考取學術寫作 7.5 以上佳績。

- 藉由大量填空題演練掌握關鍵必考學術字彙，增進聽力實力和修正拼字弱點，一舉突破 7.5 聽力關卡。

- 迅速讀懂學術長難句，優化閱讀理解和閱讀速度，搭配跳讀等閱讀技巧，時限內均能答完所有題目。

The **1.** _____ final boss of the *Octopath Traveler*, Galdera the Fallen presents a **2.** _____ huge challenge for most players. To defeat the final boss, **3.** _____ in numerous skills and thorough knowledge of the game design are required. The final boss includes two phases. During the first phase, it consists of HP 500,000 that **4.** _____ most players, leading them to comment on that wall that "We have created the most difficult boss so far". The first phase of the final boss has a huge **5.** _____ with numerous **6.** _____ and they will get **7.** _____ over time. **8.** _____ of its resistant to magic also changes during the combat. The final boss of the second phase is even more challenging than that of the first. The boss will be **9.** _____ by 99 **10.** _____ protection shields that make any attack **11.** _____ unless the protection has been broken. The boss during this stage also has several **12.** _____, but contrary to the tentacles of the first stage, they will not **13.** _____. Apart from above-mentioned challenges, there are other things that will make gamers **14.** _____ along the way. The team's **15.** _____ will be immensely **16.** _____ by the final boss, making most players abdicate. Some have come up with ways by making even higher level, reaching an average of LV 85 to beat the boss, but it's a win by a nose...

For game designers, to reach extremely high LVs has never been their intentions. A quick glance in the **17.** _____ from the official game guide book can reveal the true story. Unless there are a huge **18.** _____ in LV, say 20, figures of the character are quite close. Players have to think outside the box, instead of **19.** _____ on getting higher LVs. Further evidence from several videos solidifies the theory. With the same **20.** _____ for the team, players are able to defeat the boss with an average of LV 60-65, upending some players' viewpoints of beating the ultimate boss.

Without a complete understanding about the skills of each character, it's highly unlikely to **21.** _____ the ultimate boss. Some gamers have preconceived notions that certain characters are quite worthless, and that makes characters such as Scholar, take too much of the **22.** _____. Since Scholar has much more appealing storyline, that makes it an even better pick. However, to beat the final boss requires a team effort, so players do need to be adept at operating all 8 characters and play equally well to win the game....

Take Hunter for example, it has **Leghold Trap** that can offer the team a few more rounds to **23.** _____ the powerful strike or to **24.** _____ the team with supply and get ready. **Leghold Trap** moves the boss action to the end, making the team pre-empt. Hunter also has a unique talent that is rarely used, but presents a powerful challenge for the boss. Hunter has a capture skill that can even **25.** _____ the small boss from the side story or the maze. One particular boss can **26.** _____ damage of 50,000 in a single hit to the first phrase of the final boss, one-tenth of the boss' HP....

Starseer, though having been often overlooked, has several skills

目次 CONTENTS

IELTS READING Test 3

Test 1

篇章概述

01

幸運所扮演的影響力以及個人努力和創造機會的重要性
包含了常見的配對題搭配摘要填空的設計，建議可以採取
順答的方式進行答題。

02

從電影的角度切入並探討生物學中魚的架構
包含了圖表題、判斷題和填空題，可以採取順讀先答判斷
題，再答圖表題＋短摘要題。

03

包含了配對完成句子題＋配對題＋判斷題，這篇的難度算
是 test 1 中最難的一篇，採取順答策略，並且同步答配
對題＋判斷題，最後答完成句子題，時間才夠。

READING PASSAGE 1
You should spend about 20 minutes on **Questions 1-13**, which are based on Reading Passage 1 below.

The Role of Luck, Personal Endeavors, and Create One's Own Luck

A. Luck does play a pivotal role in how one gets hired. In the story of the Goldman Sachs, all resumes are divided into two stacks, and one of the stacks will be put into the trash can. "The whimsical decision to toss away half the resumes is the perfect example of random chance." It has become a thing that we cannot control; however, we do not have to be pessimistic about that as long as we create our own luck.

B. When a person unexpectedly gets something envious by others, such as a lucrative job, we tend to have the sour feeling inside our body that makes us say something like "they are just lucky." It is like making that kind of statement will console our mind, so people can still feel good about themselves and move on with their lives. It's true that in a rare instance, people are lucky, but you still have the power to get the luck on your side, so stop having the sour grapes when you hear the good news from others.

C. In *Ugly Betty*, Betty and Marc have been a great assistant to their boss, but still they are stuck in the position and cannot take a great step forward. It is not like they are unlucky, but they remain in a static environment. The only way to move forward is to get promoted in the company, and still that does not happen. Another assistant, Nick, whose performance was not as good as that of Betty's or Marc's, gets far ahead than the two. Nick is now an editor with assistants. He participates in YETI, a training program that will have more opportunities and interviews at the end of the program. He is the one who creates his own luck by breaking an existing status. One has to do the current job well, and at the same time looks out for a great opportunity.

D. As a saying goes, "I'm a big believer in creating your own opportunity if no one gives you one." In *Getting There*, Anderson Cooper's job search was not a smooth sailing, and he even questioned the value of a Yale education. However, after a few unsuccessful attempts, his hard work eventually paid off.

E. A similar vein can also be found in *Desperate Housewives*, when Bree says to Lynette that "I suppose that we create our own luck." Lynette used to be a successful executive in the advertising company, but now things have changed. Lynette counters with Bree's situation by saying that "we are just not as lucky as you are.", but that is not entirely correct. Bree's success in cooking and publishing has been resting on her previous accumulated effort, so she is now enjoying the outcome. Even when she is at the driveway, money blows on her windshield, making the statement "luckier people are bound to be luckier." trustful.

F. In *First Job*, Craig Dos Santos also created his own luck when he found out he went to the wrong location. He begged the recruiter to give him another interview chance even though he did not get hired eventually. The rejection did not prevent him from going forward. Thereafter, he had a thorough preparation for the Microsoft interview. That includes reading computer science algorithms books, memorizing every brain teaser, writing paragraphs of hypothetical answers, mock interviews, and so on.

G. When people hear the news that others getting a lucrative job, they are attributing other people's successes to be purely on luck. This is clearly not true. Craig's case can refute other people's jealousy and misconceptions. Luck is not just luck. Sometimes it is blended with hard work and perseverance, two traits most people usually ignore. People are unwilling to make an effort, only hoping that Goddess of luck will be on their side. You can't simply rely on luck, and you have to make an effort. For example, Henry Cavill tells the producer of *the Witcher* that he wants the job, and he has read the book and actually a game player for the Witcher. That is, he thoroughly understands the whole concept of *the Witcher*, hoping that he can be a good interpreter of the TV series, and that makes the producer convinced. One cannot simply rely on physical attractiveness and luck and all of a sudden, a great opportunity will be handed to you.

Questions 1-4
Choose the correct letter, A, B, C, or D
Write the correct letter in boxes 1-4 on your answer sheet

1. In the first paragraph, the writer uses the story of the Goldman Sachs to show
   A. the unfairness of the hiring process
   B. the vissicitude of life
   C. the invention of selecting a great resume
   D. the role of fortune

2. In the second paragraph, what's the right mindset when hearing other people's great news?
   A. find the luck yourself
   B. find the sour grapes
   C. find the consolation from other things
   D. be cynical about it

3. In the third paragraph, why does Nick get ahead whereas Betty and Marc don't?
   A. He is more competent than the two
   B. He remains in a static environment.
   C. He has several assisants.
   D. He knows opportunities come from outside.

4. In the fifth paragraph, what can be inferred about Bree and Lynette's scenario?

   A. Lynette is not as lucky as Bree.

   B. Lynette needs to be in the driveway to get more money.

   C. Bree's success comes from hard work.

   D. Lynette needs to get the executive job back.

Questions 5-9

Look at the following statements (Questions 5-9) and the list of people below.

Match each statement with the correct people, A-G

Write the correct letter, A-G, in boxes 5-9 on your answer sheet.

NB You may use any letter more than once.

5 gets the declination
6 has a thorough preparation through familiarizing the game
7 had the doubt of a fantastic diploma
8 overshadows a person whose career used to be successful
9 overshadows previous colleagues

List of people

A Betty
B Craig Dos Santos
C Anderson Cooper
D Henry Cavill
E Marc
F Nick
G Bree

Questions 10-13

Complete the notes below

Choose ONE WORD ONLY from the passage for each answer

Write your answers in boxes 10-13 on your answer sheet.

	DESCRIPTIONS
the Witcher	● Henry Cavill can be a believable **10.**_____ because he had a thorough preparation. To make the **11.**_____ persuaded, reading the book and playing the game are the key.
First Job	● In *First Job*, Craig Dos Santos also created his own luck by begging the **12.**_____ to give him another opportunity. ● The preparation of the Microsoft interview was a living proof that he created the luck. Preparations are made up of **13.**_____ brain teaser, reading computer science algorithms books, and so on.

01｜商管＋面試

《*Getting There*》、《*First Job*》、《*The Witcher*》和《慾望師奶》

幸運所扮演的影響力以及個人努力和創造機會的重要性

　　在答題前第一個步驟是先快速掃視題目題型並快速制定答題策略，在這篇很快可以看到配對題的部分，配對題大多是依順序出題，所以採取「順答」，照文章段落順序閱讀文章並答題。

◆ **第一題**，In the first paragraph, the writer uses the story of the Goldman Sachs to show，段落中提到履歷表和招聘等，但主要提到的是 random chance，運氣如何影響聘用，其實重點在段落主題句 Luck does play a pivotal role in how one gets hired.，故**答案要選 D**，the role of fortune，其他選項均是干擾選項或不符提問所問的。

◆ **第二題**，in the second paragraph, what's the right mindset when hearing other people's great news，要注意到 the right mindset，而非段落中人們聽到時的反應，所以要刪除像是 they are just lucky 等的相關敘述。B 選項的 find the sour grapes 也顯然不對，文中雖有提到 sour feeling 和 sour grapes 但卻是在形容，而非要去尋找酸葡萄，可以先刪除 B。C 選項的 find the consolations in other things，也未提及，文中是說 It is like

Test 1

1
TEST
Reading Passage 1

2
TEST

3
TEST

4
TEST

making that kind of statement will console our mind，故也可以刪除 C。D 的 be cynical about it 顯然跟第二段文末提到的 stop having the sour grapes when you hear the good news from others 敘述表達不同，故也可以刪除 D，這題**要選的是 A**。

◆ **第三題**，in the third paragraph, why does Nick get ahead whereas Betty and Marc don't，A 選項的 he is more competent than the two，顯然與 Another assistant, Nick, whose performance was not as good as that of Betty's or Marc's, gets far ahead than the two.描述的相反，nick 之前的工作表現沒有比較好，他反而最後發展得比較好，這也是作者提到的原因，故要刪除 A 選項。He remains in a static environment 也是錯誤的敘述，It is not like they are unlucky, but they remain in a static environment.，在 static environment 的是 Betty and Marc，所以也可以刪除 B。C 選項的 he has several assisants，這部分段落中有提到，Nick is now an editor with assistants.，但這並非題問所問的，題目是詢問 get ahead 的原因。D 選項的 he knows opportunities come from outside，跟段落敘述像是 He is the one who creates his own luck by breaking an existing status.，故**答案要選 D**。

◆ **第四題**，可以先跳過第四段先閱讀第五段並答題，in the fifth paragraph, what can be inferred about Bree and Lynette's scenario，選項 A，Lynette is not as lucky as Bree.，文中僅提到 Lynette counters with Bree's situation by saying that "we are just not as lucky as you are." but that is not entirely correct.，由此可以先刪除 A。選項 B，Lynette needs to be in the driveway to get more money，文中有提到 Even when she is at the driveway, money blows on her windshield，指的是 Bree，且無法判斷出 Lynette 也要在 driveway 以獲取更多的錢，也可以刪除 B。選項 C，Bree's success comes from hard work，這點跟 Bree's success in cooking and publishing has been resting on her previous accumulated effort 吻合（如果非常確定的話，是可以略過 D 選項以節省時間），答案要**選 C**。選項 D，Lynette needs to get the executive job back. 文中僅說 Lynette used to be a successful executive in the advertising company，故無法判斷。

◆ **第五題**，接著來到第六段，gets the declination，這部分可以對應到 He begged the recruiter to give him another interview chance even though **he did not get hired** eventually. The **rejection** did not prevent him from going forward.，可以得知他被拒絕了，故答案要選 **B**。

◆ **第六題**，接著讀到 he had a thorough preparation for the Microsoft interview... 等等，這部分對應到第六題的 has a thorough preparation **through familiarizing the game**，但僅有前面的部分吻合，through familiarizing the game 的部分

Test 1

1 TEST
Reading Passage 1

2 TEST

3 TEST

4 TEST

不合，接續讀到 Henry Cavill tells the producer of *the Witcher* that he wants the job, and he has read the book and actually a game player for the Witcher.，actually a game player 跟這部分吻合，故要選 **D**。

◆ **第七題**，答完第六題後會發現沒有第七題的答題線索，這時可以回到剛才跳過的第四段落找答案，and he even questioned the value of a Yale education 和 had the doubt of a fantastic diploma 敘述吻合，故**答案要選 C**。

◆ **第八題**，overshadows a person whose career used to be successful，這點可以回想到剛才讀過的 Bree 那段的部分，Lynette used to be a successful executive in the advertising company, but now things have changed.，Bree 現在反而發展得比較好了，故**答案要選 G**。

◆ **第九題**，overshadows previous colleagues，可以馬上想到剛才讀到的 Nick，如果沒有的話也可以重新再掃描訊息，Nick 的表現 overshadow Betty 和 Marc，故**答案要選 F**。

◆ **第十題和十一題**，Henry Cavill can be a believable **10.**_____ because he had a thorough preparation. To make the **11.**_____ persuaded, reading the book and playing the game are the key.，這部分可以由表格中的 the Witcher 快速定位到最後一段，**believable** 可以對應到 **convinced**，he thoroughly understands the whole concept of the Witcher, hoping that he can be a good interpreter of the TV series, and that makes the producer convinced.，故可以在這句中找尋答案，他能成為可信的詮釋者，故答案要選 **interpreter**，而第 11 題也可以由 convinced 對應到 persuaded 得知是 to make the producer 信服，故答案是 **producer**。

- 第十二題，In *First Job*, Craig Dos Santos also created his own luck by begging the **12.**_____ to give him another opportunity.，可以對應到 He begged the recruiter to give him another interview chance even though he did not get hired eventually.答案很明顯是 **recruiter**。

- 第十三題，The preparation of the Microsoft interview was a living proof that he created the luck. Preparations are made up of **13.**_____ brain teaser, reading computer science algorithms books, and so on.，這部分可以對應到 That includes reading computer science algorithms books, memorizing every brain teaser, writing paragraphs of hypothetical answers, mock interviews, and so on.表舉例的部分，要注意的點是 of 後要加名詞或 Ving，原文段落中剛好也是 memorizing，這題答案為 **memorizing**。

聽讀整合 TEST 1 P1

Luck does play a **1.**_____ role in how one gets hired. In the story of the Goldman Sachs, all **2.**_____ are divided into two stacks, and one of the stacks will be put into the trash can. "The **3.**_____ decision to toss away half the resumes is the perfect example of **4.**_____ chance." ...When a person **5.**_____ gets something envious by others, such as a **6.**_____ job, we tend to have the sour feeling inside our body that makes us say something like "they are just lucky." It is like making that kind of **7.**_____ will **8.**_____ our mind, so people can still feel good about themselves and move on with their lives...

In *Ugly Betty*, Betty and Marc have been a great **9.**_____ to their boss, but still they are stuck in the **10.**_____ and cannot take a great step forward. It is not like they are unlucky, but they remain in a **11.**_____ environment. The only way to move forward is to get **12.**_____ in the company, and still that does not happen. Another assistant, Nick, whose **13.**_____ was not as good as that of Betty's or Marc's, gets far ahead than the two. Nick is now an **14.**_____ with assistants. He participates in YETI, a training program that will have more **15.**_____ and interviews at the end of the program. He is the one who creates his own luck by breaking an **16.**_____ status. One has to do the current job well, and at the same time looks out for a great opportunity. ...As a saying goes, "I'm a big **17.**_____ in creating your own opportunity if no one gives you one." In *Getting There*, Anderson Cooper's job search was not a **18.**_____ sailing, and he even questioned the value of a Yale education. However, after a few unsuccessful **19.**_____, his hard work eventually paid off.

A similar vein can also be found in *Desperate Housewives*, when Bree says to Lynette that "I suppose that we create our own luck." Lynette used to be a successful **20.**_____ in the **21.**_____ company, but now things have changed. Lynette counters with Bree's situation by saying that "we are just not as lucky as you are.", but that is not entirely correct. Bree's success in cooking and publishing has been resting on her previous **22.**_____ effort, so she is now enjoying the **23.**_____. Even when she is at the driveway, money blows on her **24.**_____, making the statement "luckier people are bound to be luckier." trustful.

In *First Job*, Craig Dos Santos also created his own luck when he found out he went to the wrong location. He begged the **25.**_____ to give him another interview chance even though he did not get hired eventually. The **26.**_____ did not prevent him from going forward. Thereafter, he had a thorough **27.**_____ for the Microsoft interview. That includes reading computer science **28.**_____ books, **29.**_____ every brain teaser, writing paragraphs of **30.**_____ answers, mock interviews, and so on.

...Craig's case can refute other people's jealousy and misconceptions. Luck is not just luck. Sometimes it is blended with hard work and **31.**_____, two traits most people usually ignore... For example, Henry Cavill tells the producer of *the Witcher* that he wants the job, and he has read the book and actually a game player for the Witcher. That is, he thoroughly understands the whole concept of *the Witcher*, hoping that he can be a good **32.**_____ of the TV series, and that makes the producer convinced...

Test 1

1
TEST
Reading Passage 1

2
TEST

3
TEST

4
TEST

中譯和影子跟讀　　　　　　　　　　　　　　🔘 MP3 013

A. Luck does play a pivotal role in how one gets hired. In the story of the Goldman Sachs, all resumes are divided into two stacks, and one of the stacks will be put into the trash can. "The whimsical decision to toss away half the resumes is the perfect example of random chance." It has become a thing that we cannot control; however, we do not have to be pessimistic about that as long as we create our own luck.

幸運確實在一個人獲得聘用上扮演要角。在高盛公司的故事中，所有的履歷會分成兩堆，而其中一堆會被丟到垃圾桶。「這個異想天開將一半的履歷丟掉的決定就是隨機運氣的極佳例子」。這已經成了我們所無法控制的事情了，然而，只要我們創造自我的幸運，我們就不用因此而感到悲觀。

B. When a person unexpectedly gets something envious by others, such as a lucrative job, we tend to have the sour feeling inside our body that makes us say something like "they are just lucky." It is like making that kind of statement will console our mind, so people can still feel good about themselves and move on with their lives. It's true that in a rare instance, people are lucky, but you still have the power to get the luck on your side, so stop having the sour grapes when you hear the good news from others.

當一個人出乎意料之外地獲得了其他人稱羨的事物，例如一份賺錢的工作，我們體內易於有種酸的滋味讓我們述說著「他們只是比較幸運」。彷彿是那個說法讓我們心靈能得到撫慰，所以人們仍可以自我感覺良好，然後繼續我們的生活。千真萬確的是，在極少的例子中，人們是幸運的，但是你還是有著讓幸運站在你這邊的力量，所以在你從他人那裡聽到好消息時，別再有酸葡萄心理了。

C. In *Ugly Betty*, Betty and Marc have been a great assistant to their boss, but still they are stuck in the position and cannot take a great step forward. It is not like they are unlucky, but they remain in a static environment. The only way to move forward is to get promoted in the company, and still that does not happen. Another assistant, Nick, whose performance was not as good as that of Betty's or Marc's, gets far ahead than the two. Nick is now an editor with assistants. He participates in YETI, a training program that will have more opportunities and interviews at the end of the program. He is the one who creates his own luck by breaking an existing status. One has to do the current job well, and at the same time looks out for a great opportunity.

在《醜女貝蒂》中，對他們的老闆來說，貝蒂和馬克一直都是很棒的助理，但是他們仍舊在職位上裹足不前，且無法向前大步邁進。這並不是意謂著它們不幸運，只是它們仍舊是待在一個靜止的環境中。唯一向前邁進的辦法就是在公司內獲得晉升，而這件事卻沒有發生。另一位助理，尼克過去的表現並沒有貝蒂或馬克好，卻比他們兩個人都更平步青雲。尼克現在是個編輯且有助理們。他參加了 YETI，一個訓練計畫，讓參予者在計畫結束後有更多的機會和面試。尼克就是位打破現有狀態以獲取自己幸運的人。人是必須要做好本職工作並且同時向外尋求更棒的機會。

D. As a saying goes, "I'm a big believer in creating your own opportunity if no one gives you one." In *Getting There*, Anderson Cooper's job search was not a smooth sailing, and he even questioned the value of a Yale education. However, after a few unsuccessful attempts, his hard work eventually paid off.

俗話說，「如果沒有任何人給你機會的話，我深信你是要替自己創造機會的那個人」。在《勝利並非事事順利》，安德森·庫柏的求職並非一帆風順，而且他甚至開始質疑著耶魯大學學歷的價值。然而，在幾次不成功的嘗試之後，他的努力最終有了回報。

E. A similar vein can also be found in *Desperate Housewives*, when Bree says to Lynette that "I suppose that we create our own luck." Lynette used to be a successful executive in the advertising company, but now things have changed. Lynette counters with Bree's situation by saying that "we are just not as lucky as you are.", but that is not entirely correct. Bree's success in cooking and publishing has been resting on her previous accumulated effort, so she is now enjoying the outcome. Even when she is at the driveway, money blows on her windshield, making the statement "luckier people are bound to be luckier." trustful.

在《慾望師奶》中也能找到相似點，當布里對琳奈特說道「我認為我們應該是要創造自己的幸運」。琳奈特過去曾是廣告公司成功的高階主管，但是事過境遷了。琳奈特回應布里的狀況說道，「我們只是沒你那麼幸運而已」，但是這個論述完全不符合實情。布里在烹飪和出版的成功一直都是仰賴著她早先累積的努力，所以她現在能享受成果。即使當她在車道上，都有錢吹到她的擋風玻璃上頭，這讓論述「幸運的人一定會更為幸運」令人感到真實。

F. In *First Job*, Craig Dos Santos also created his own luck when he found out he went to the wrong location. He begged the recruiter to give him another interview chance even though he did not get hired eventually. The rejection did not prevent him from going forward. Thereafter, he had a thorough preparation for the Microsoft interview. That includes reading computer science algorithms books, memorizing every brain teaser, writing paragraphs of hypothetical answers, mock interviews, and so on.

在《首份工作》，奎格・山道士亦創造了自己的幸運，當他察覺到自己走錯地點時。他乞求招聘員給他額外的面試機會，即使他最終並未獲得聘用。受到拒絕並未阻止他繼續前進。後來，他對於微軟的面試有了透徹的準備。那包含了閱讀電腦科學演算的書籍、背誦每個 brain teaser，以及撰寫假設性的段落答案、模仿面試等等的。

G. When people hear the news that others getting a lucrative job, they are attributing other people's successes to be purely on luck. This is clearly not true. Craig's case can refute other people's jealousy and misconceptions. Luck is not just luck. Sometimes it is blended with hard work and perseverance, two traits most people usually ignore. People are unwilling to make an effort, only hoping that Goddess of luck will be on their side. You can't simply rely on luck, and you have to make an effort. For example, Henry Cavill tells the producer of the Witcher that he wants the job, and he has read the book and actually a game player for the Witcher. That is, he thoroughly understands the whole concept of the Witcher, hoping that he can be a good interpreter of the TV series, and that makes the producer convinced. One cannot simply rely on physical attractiveness and luck and all of a sudden, a great opportunity will be handed to you.

當人們聽到其他人獲取賺錢的工作時，他們都將別人的成功歸因於幸運。這顯然是不正確的。奎格的例子就能駁斥其他人的忌妒和錯誤觀念。幸運不僅是幸運。有時候參雜著努力付出和毅力，兩項大多數人都會忽略的特質。人們不願意付出努力，僅希望幸運女神終將站在他們那邊。你不能只是仰賴幸運，而是必須要付出努力。亨利·卡維爾告訴獵魔士的製作人他想要這份工作，而且他已經閱讀了這本書籍，實際上亦是獵魔士這款遊戲的玩家。也就是說，他對獵魔士的完整概念有著透徹的了解，並期許自己能夠成為這部電視劇的良好詮釋者，而那樣的說法讓製作人感到信服。一個人顯然無法仰賴外在吸引力和幸運，而突然之間，一個很棒的機會就遞交到你手中。

You should spend about 20 minutes on Questions 14-27 which are based on Reading Passage 2 below.

Mermaid Legend:
From the Film's Perspectives to the Anatomy of Fish

A. During his childhood, Zhi was punished by his mother's boyfriend for cutting a fish wire. While the yacht was still sailing, Zhi had been deliberately pushed by the guy, making him fall into the ocean. The young Zhi did not know how to swim, making his mother increasingly worried. Due to Zhi's kindheartedness, he was eventually saved by a big fish, asserting that he proclaimed to other witnesses on the shore who had found him. However, bystanders on the shore knew that he was just recovered from the drowning; therefore, they did not take his words seriously.

B. Pretty soon, Zhi is now a handsome grown-up teaching sports at high school. Still he does not know how to swim. During the voyage of the school trip, several students were heading of throwing a girl into the water by counting from one to three, and they did. A P.E. teacher who does not know how to swim does not convince those students. This led to a push from the crowd, causing Zhi to sink in.

READING PASSAGE 2

You should spend about 20 minutes on **Questions 14-27**, which are based on Reading Passage 2 below.

Mermaid Legend:
From the Film's Perspectives to the Anatomy of Fish

A. During his childhood, Zhi was punished by his mother's boyfriend for cutting a fish wire. While the yacht was still sailing, Zhi had been deliberately pushed by the guy, making him fall into the ocean. The young Zhi did not know how to swim, making his mother increasingly worried. Due to Zhi's kindheartedness, he was eventually saved by a big fish, a saying that he proclaimed to other witnesses on the shore who had found him. However, bystanders on the shore knew that he was just recovered from the drowning; therefore, they did not take his words seriously.

B. Pretty soon, Zhi is now a handsome grown-up teaching sports at high school. Still he does not know how to swim. During the voyage of the school trip, several students were heckling of throwing a girl into the water by counting from one to three, and they did. A P.E. teacher who does not know how to swim does not convince those students. This led to a push from the crowd, causing Zhi to sink in

Test 1

1

TEST

Reading Passage 2

TEST 2

TEST 3

TEST 4

the ocean. It was not until later that the water remained static did those students know that Zhi truly does not know how to swim.

C. Luckily, for Zhi, he had been saved by a mermaid who deemed that it was a serendipitous encounter. A wriggling of the caudal fin by the mermaid can be clearly seen in the scene. However, saving Zhi requires using the pearl that the mermaid possesses, and it is the essential item for the mermaid to swim back to the ocean. She has to get the pearl back, and this has led to a gripping development of the movie.

D. The mermaid is then the incarnation of Xiao Mei, who is now a high school student that Zhi is currently teaching. During the biology class, the teacher is teaching the subject of fish anatomy with English terms on the black board. While teaching, she finds a scene that is considered nuisance that disturbs her teaching, a high school hunk who is daydreaming during the class. After getting caught by the lecturer, he blurts out something that makes Xiao Mei laugh. This soon makes the instructor unpleasant, and she decides to punish Xiao Mei by pointing to all the blank parts of fish anatomy on the black board. Things turn out to be quite unexpected as Xiao Mei gets all the answers correct in a few seconds, and that makes all of them astounded. Xiao Mei then gets accolades by the teacher that she is well-prepared for the class. But Xiao Mei is, in fact, a fish. Of course, she understands all her body parts.

E.   Unlike human beings, who are reliant on the lung to breathe, fish depend on the gill to get the oxygen from the water, and eventually make the air exchange. The pectoral fins are the closest to the gill, and other than its position, the pectoral fins are a pair that is located by both sides of the fish body. The function of the pectoral fins is said to be analogous to that of the forelimbs of four-feet animals, and they are related to fish's maneuverability.

F.   Pelvic fins are also paired, and are situated below the pectoral fins. The function of the pelvic fins is like car brakes in the car, so they are related to the stability of the fish, and in a rare instance, pelvic fins are positioned in front of the pectoral fins.

G.   Dorsal fins and adipose fins are both located on the back of the fish, so it is easily recognized. Also noteworthy is the fact that adipose fins are remarkably smaller than those of the dorsal, and their functions remain a puzzle. "In a 2011 leaked information, adipose fins are related to sense, such as touch and sound, and water pressure." Dorsal fins keep the fish from undulations, making them not vacillate.

H. Between pelvic fins and caudal fins, it's anal fins. Anal fins are also called cloacal fins, which have the function of stabilizing the fish.

I. Aside from those above-mentioned functions, fins have other purposes, too. Fins can also be used as the delivery for sperm, and caudal fins have the function of stupefying the prey. That is quite a common function that we know about tail fins that are functioned as forward moment and stability. In addition, in some species, there are spines hidden in the dorsal fins that can insert venom into the prey. Pectoral fins also have distinctive functions that give the fish animated lifting to capture flying fish. The anatomy of fish is not that hard to grasp. If you were a high school student, you obviously wouldn't need the flair of Xiao Mei to impress your biology lecturer or crack IELTS reading parts.

Questions 14-19

Label the diagram below

Choose NO MORE THAN TWO WORDS from the passage for each answer.

Write your answers in boxes 14-19 on your answer sheet.

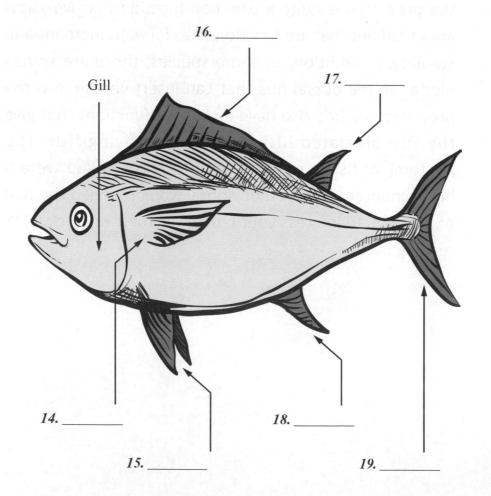

16. _____

17. _____

Gill

14. _____

15. _____

18. _____

19. _____

Questions 20-23

Complete the summary below

Choose No More Than One Word from the passage for each answer

Write your answers in boxes 20-23 on your answer sheet.

The function of **20.**_____ fins stays enigmatic. Fish will not **21.**_____ due to dorsal fins' function of maintaining water movement.

Fins even possess the function for **22.**_____ shipment. The quarry will get **23.**_____ .

Questions 24-27

Do the following statements agree with the information given in the Reading Passage 2

In boxes 24-27 on your answer sheet, write

> **TRUE**- if the statement agrees with the information
> **FALSE**- if the statement contradicts the information
> **NOT GIVEN**- if there is no information on this

24. Bystanders believed that Zhi had been saved by a big fish.
25. During the voyage of the school trip, the mermaid made the water stationary to fool those students that Zhi can't swim.
26. The mermaid does need the highly prized gem to swim back to the ocean.
27. It's not surprising that Xiao Mei answers the anatomy of fish correctly because she is a fish.

解析

02 ｜生物學＋電影
《第六感奇緣之人魚傳說》
從電影的角度切入並探討生物學中魚的架構

　　在答題前第一個步驟是先快速掃視題目題型並快速制定答題策略，在這篇很快可以看到有圖表題、短摘要題和判斷題，可以採取順讀先答判斷題，再答圖表題＋短摘要題。

◆ **第 24 題**，可以藉由題目的關鍵字 Bystanders，定位到第一段結尾 However, **bystanders** on the shore knew that he was just recovered from the drowning; therefore, they did not take his words seriously.，敘述中可以知道旁觀者們並沒有把他的話當真，所以跟題目所述 bystanders believed that Zhi had been saved by a big fish 不一致，故答案要選 **False**。

◆ **第 25 題**，During the voyage of the school trip, **the mermaid made the water stationary to fool those students** that Zhi can't swim，可以由 During the voyage of the school trip，定位到第二段第二句，快速看到段落結尾 It was not until later that the water remained static did those students know that Zhi truly does not know how to swim.，學生之後才意識到他不會游，但沒有題目所述 **the mermaid made the water stationary to fool those students** 的部分，故要選 **Not**

Given。（不放心的話可以繼續看到第三段第一句有美人魚出現的部分跟整個段落，在第 3 題和第 2 題間找訊息，可以知道沒有這樣的敘述）。

◆ **第 26 題**，可以由 the mermaid does need the highly prized gem to swim back to the ocean 中的 the highly prized gem 定位到 However, saving Zhi requires using **the pearl** that the mermaid possesses，the highly prized gem 就是 **pearl**，以及次一句 and it is the essential item for the mermaid to swim back to the ocean.，由這些綜合訊息可以得知題目所述是正確的，**答案要選 True**。

◆ **第 27 題**，it's not surprising that Xiao Mei answers the anatomy of fish correctly because she is a fish，可以定位到第四段最後一句，But Xiao Mei is, in fact, a fish. Of course, she understands all her body parts.，故**答案要選 True**。

◆ **第 20 題**，The function of 20.＿＿＿＿＿＿＿ fins stays enigmatic.，可以藉由 enigmatic 定位到 Also noteworthy is the fact that adipose fins are remarkably smaller than those of the dorsal, and their functions remain a puzzle.，**enigmatic** 指的就是 **puzzle**，所以可以得知指的鰭是 adipose，故答案是 **adipose**。

◆ **第 21 題**，Fish will not 21._____ due to dorsal fins' function of maintaining water movement.，water movement 可以對應到 Dorsal fins keep the fish from undulations, making them not vacillate.中的 **undulations**，所以可以知道 fish will not vacillate，答案為 **vacillate**。

◆ **第 22 題**，Fins even possess the function for 22._____ shipment.，可以藉由 shipment 定位到 Fins can also be used as the delivery for sperm，shipment 指的就是 **delivery**，所以可以得知是用於傳遞精子，**答案為 sperm**。

◆ **第 23 題**，The quarry will get 23._____.，可以藉由 quarry 定位回 caudal fins have the function of stupefying the prey.，quarry 指的就是 prey，故答案很明顯是 **stupefying**，但是要根據語法做變化，get 後面要用形容詞當補語，所以要將 stupefying 改成 stupefied，**答案為 stupefied**。

◆ **第 14 題**，觀看圖表可以看到是位在鰓附近的位置，這部分可以定位到 The **pectoral fins** are the closest to **the gill**, and other than its position, the pectoral fins are a pair that is located by both sides of the fish body.，所以**第 14 題**的答案是 **pectoral fin**。

◆ **第 15 題**，pelvic fins are also paired, and are situated below the pectoral fins.腹鰭也是成對，而且位於胸鰭下方。所以第 15 題的答案是 **pelvic fin**。

◆ **第 16 題**，就不像是第 15 題那樣順著敘述，而是夾雜介紹兩種鰭，dorsal fins and adipose fins are both located on the back of the fish, so it is easily recognized. Also noteworthy is the fact that adipose fins are remarkably smaller than those of the dorsal, and their functions remain a puzzle. "In a 2011 leaked information, adipose fins are related to sense, such as touch and sound, and water pressure." Dorsal fins keep the fish from undulations, making them not vacillate.，但是可以由後面的，脂鰭比起背鰭顯得更為小些判斷出**第 16 題**是 **dorsal fins**。

◆ **第 17 題**，可以由上一題的位置順序反推出答案是 **adipose fin**。

◆ **第 19 題**，A wriggling of the caudal fin by the mermaid can be clearly seen in the scene.這部分是第一次提到尾鰭的部分，而在後面的敘述中僅提到尾鰭的其他功用但是沒有提到位置，不過也能用這部份去判斷出這題答案是 **caudal fin**。

◆ **第 18 題**，確定尾鰭的位置後就能藉由 between pelvic fins and caudal fins, it's anal fins.得知這題的答案是 **anal fin**。

During his childhood, Zhi was **1.**_____ by his mother's boyfriend for cutting a fish wire. While the **2.**_____ was still sailing, Zhi had been deliberately pushed by the guy, making him fall into the ocean. Due to Zhi's **3.**_____, he was eventually saved by a big fish, a saying that he proclaimed to other **4.**_____ on the shore who had found him. However, **5.**_____ on the shore knew that he was just **6.**_____ from the drowning; therefore, they did not take his words seriously. A P.E. teacher who does not know how to swim does not convince those students. This led to a push from the crowd, causing Zhi to sink in the ocean. Luckily, for Zhi, he had been saved by a **7.**_____ who deemed that it was a **8.**_____ encounter. A **9.**_____ of the caudal fin by the mermaid can be clearly seen in the scene. However, saving Zhi requires using the **10.**_____ that the mermaid possesses... The mermaid is then the **11.**_____ of Xiao Mei, who is now a high school student that Zhi is currently teaching. During the **12.**_____ class, the teacher is teaching the subject of fish **13.**_____ with English terms on the black board. While teaching, she finds a scene that is considered **14.**_____ that disturbs her teaching, a high school hunk who is daydreaming during the class.... Things turn out to be quite **15.**_____ as Xiao Mei gets all the answers correct in a few seconds, and that makes all of them astounded. Xiao Mei then gets **16.**_____ by the teacher that she is well-prepared for the class. But Xiao Mei is, in fact, a fish.

Unlike human beings, who are **17.**_____ on the lung to breathe, fish depend on the gill to get the **18.**_____ from the water, and eventually make the air exchange. The pectoral fins are the closest to the **19.**_____, and other than its position, the pectoral fins are a pair that is located by both sides of the fish body. The function of the pectoral fins is said to be **20.**_____ to that of the forelimbs of four-feet animals, and they are related to fish's **21.**_____. The function of the pelvic fins is like car brakes in the car, so they are related to the **22.**_____ of the fish, and in a rare instance, pelvic fins are positioned in front of the pectoral fins. Also noteworthy is the fact that adipose fins are remarkably smaller than those of the dorsal, and their functions remain a **23.**_____. "In a 2011 leaked information, adipose fins are related to **24.**_____, such as touch and sound, and water **25.**_____." Dorsal fins keep the fish from **26.**_____, making them not vacillate. Aside from those above-mentioned functions, fins have other purposes, too. Fins can also be used as the **27.**_____ for sperm, and caudal fins have the function of **28.**_____ the prey. That is quite a common function that we know about tail fins that are functioned as forward moment and stability. In addition, in some species, there are spines **29.**_____ in the dorsal fins that can insert **30.**_____ into the prey. Pectoral fins also have **31.**_____ functions that give the fish animated lifting to capture flying fish. The anatomy of fish is not that hard to grasp. If you were a high school student, you obviously wouldn't need the **32.**_____ of Xiao Mei to impress your biology lecturer or crack IELTS reading parts.

A. During his childhood, Zhi was punished by his mother's boyfriend for cutting a fish wire. While the yacht was still sailing, Zhi had been deliberately pushed by the guy, making him fall into the ocean. The young Zhi did not know how to swim, making his mother increasingly worried. Due to Zhi's kindheartedness, he was eventually saved by a big fish, a saying that he proclaimed to other witnesses on the shore who had found him. However, bystanders on the shore knew that he was just recovered from the drowning; therefore, they did not take his words seriously.

在他小時候，志因為剪斷魚線而受到他母親男友的處罰。當遊艇仍在行駛時，志被該男子故意一推，他因此跌入了海中。年幼的志並不知道如何游泳，這讓他母親感到與日俱增的擔憂。由於志的善心，他最終被一條大魚所救，這是他向岸上其他發現他的目擊者所宣稱的陳述。然而，在岸上的旁觀者們知道，志不過是剛從溺水中康復過來，因此，他們並未將志的言論當真。

B. Pretty soon, Zhi is now a handsome grown-up teaching sports at high school. Still he does not know how to swim. During the voyage of the school trip, several students were heckling of throwing a girl into the water by counting from one to three, and they did. A P.E. teacher who does not know how to swim does not convince those students. This led to a push from the crowd, causing Zhi to sink in the ocean. It was not until later that the water remained static did those students know that Zhi truly does not know how to swim.

時間過得很快，志現在是位在高中教體育的英俊成年人了。他仍舊不會游泳。在學校郊遊的旅途中，幾個學生起鬨要將一個女生丟入水中，從數一至三，最終將其丟入水裡。一位體育老師不會游泳無法說服那些學生。這促成一群人的推擠，進而導致志沉到海裡。一直到水面維持靜止不動，那些學生才知道志是真的不會游泳。

C. Luckily, for Zhi, he had been saved by a mermaid who deemed that it was a serendipitous encounter. A wriggling of the caudal fin by the mermaid can be clearly seen in the scene. However, saving Zhi requires using the pearl that the mermaid possesses, and it is the essential item for the mermaid to swim back to the ocean. She has to get the pearl back, and this has led to a gripping development of the movie.

幸運的是，志被一條美人魚所救，那條美人魚認為這是個奇緣。美人魚蠕動尾鰭在該場景中清晰可見。然而，拯救志需要使用美人魚所持有的珍珠，而這個珍珠也是美人魚游回海洋的重要物品。她必須要拿回珍珠，這也促成了電影中扣人心弦的發展。

D. The mermaid is then the incarnation of Xiao Mei, who is now a high school student that Zhi is currently teaching. During the biology class, the teacher is teaching the subject of fish anatomy with English terms on the black board. While teaching, she finds a scene that is considered nuisance that disturbs her teaching, a high school hunk who is daydreaming during the class. After getting caught by the lecturer, he blurts out something that makes Xiao Mei laugh. This soon makes the instructor unpleasant, and she decides to punish Xiao Mei by pointing to all the blank parts of fish anatomy on the black board. Things turn out to be quite unexpected as Xiao Mei gets all the answers correct in a few seconds, and that makes all of them astounded. Xiao Mei then gets accolades by the teacher that she is well-prepared for the class. But Xiao Mei is, in fact, a fish. Of course, she understands all her body parts.

隨後美人魚就是小美的化身，一位志現在在高中所教授的學

Test 1

1 TEST
Reading Passage 2

2 TEST

3 TEST

4 TEST

生。在生物課的時候，老師在黑板上正以英語專有名詞教授魚的解剖構造的主題。在授課時，老師發現一個擾人授課的景象，該景象也被視為是討人厭的事情，一位高中帥哥在課堂中做白日夢。在被授課老師抓到後，他突然講了讓小美捧腹而笑的話。這隨即讓指導老師感到不悅，並且決定要懲罰小美，並指著在黑板上頭，魚的解剖構造空白挖空處。事情的轉變卻全然出乎意料之外，因為小美在幾秒內就將所有答案答對，此舉讓他們所有人都感到驚訝萬分。小美接著受到老師的讚許，老師稱讚她是個準備充分的學生。但是，小美實際上是條魚。她當然了解她自己的身體構造。

E. Unlike human beings, who are reliant on the lung to breathe, fish depend on the gill to get the oxygen from the water, and eventually make the air exchange. The pectoral fins are the closest to the gill, and other than its position, the pectoral fins are a pair that is located by both sides of the fish body. The function of the pectoral fins is said to be analogous to that of the forelimbs of four-feet animals, and they are related to fish's maneuverability.

跟仰賴肺來呼吸的人類不同的是，魚依靠鰓以獲取水中的氧氣，而最終進行氣體交換。胸鰭的位置就是最靠近鰓的，而除了它的位置外，胸鰭是成對的，且位於魚體的兩側。胸鰭的功用據說與四足動物的前肢的功能是同源的，而胸鰭也跟魚的機動性有關。

F. Pelvic fins are also paired, and are situated below the pectoral fins. The function of the pelvic fins is like car brakes in the car, so they are related to the stability of the fish, and in a rare instance, pelvic fins are positioned in front of the pectoral fins.

腹鰭也是成對，而且位於胸鰭下方。腹鰭的功用就像是車子的煞車，所以它們跟魚的穩定性有關，且在罕見的例子中，腹鰭位於胸鰭的前方。

G. Dorsal fins and adipose fins are both located on the back of the fish, so it is easily recognized. Also noteworthy is the fact that adipose fins are remarkably smaller than those of the dorsal, and their functions remain a puzzle. "In a 2011 leaked information, adipose fins are related to sense, such as touch and sound, and water pressure." Dorsal fins keep the fish from undulations, making them not vacillate.

背鰭和脂鰭均位於魚的背部，所以很容易辨識出。也值得注意的是，脂鰭比起背鰭顯得更為小些，而且脂鰭的功用仍舊是個謎團。「在 2011 年所揭露的資訊中，脂鰭與感官有關聯，例如觸覺、聲音和水壓」。背鰭讓魚免於受水的波動的影響，使魚不會擺動。

Test 1

1
TEST
Reading Passage 2

2
TEST

3
TEST

4
TEST

H. Between pelvic fins and caudal fins, it's anal fins. Anal fins are also called cloacal fins, which have the function of stabilizing the fish.

位於腹鰭和尾鰭中間的是臀鰭。臀鰭也稱作臀鰭（cloacal），具有使魚平衡的功用。

I. Aside from those above-mentioned functions, fins have other purposes, too. Fins can also be used as the delivery for sperm, and caudal fins have the function of stupefying the prey. That is quite a common function that we know about tail fins that are functioned as forward moment and stability. In addition, in some species, there are spines hidden in the dorsal fins that can insert venom into the prey. Pectoral fins also have distinctive functions that give the fish animated lifting to capture flying fish. The anatomy of fish is not that hard to grasp. If you were a high school student, you obviously wouldn't need the flair of Xiao Mei to impress your biology lecturer or crack IELTS reading parts.

除了那些上述所提到的功用之外，魚鰭還有其他的功用在。魚鰭也能夠用於精子的傳遞，而尾鰭有使獵物昏沉的功用。那是我們對尾鰭所知的一項相當普遍的功用，其也能用於移動向前和穩定性。此外，在有些物種中，背鰭裡隱藏了刺，能用於將毒液注入獵物體內。胸鰭有著顯著的功用能讓魚活躍的升起以捕獲飛魚。魚的結構並沒有想像中那麼難捉摸。如果你是個高中生，你顯然不需要小美的天賦以獲得生物老師的青睞或是破解雅思閱讀的部分。

READING PASSAGE 3
You should spend about 20 minutes on Questions 28-40
which are based on Reading Passage 3 below.

Business School Cases:
What Else Do You Still Need to Know About Money

A. "All of us had an ample share of the treasure, and used it wisely or foolishly, according to our natures," "Captain Smollett is now retired from the sea. Gray not only saved his money, but being suddenly smit with the desire to rise, also studied his profession, and he is now mate and part owner of a fine-rigged ship, married besides, and the father of a family. As for Ben Gunn, he got a thousand pounds, which he spent or lost in three weeks, or to be more exact, in nineteen days."

B. These quotes have been closely linked to one's spending habits and use of money. These also correspond to several notions mentioning in one of the bestsellers, The Wealth Elite. It is not about the inheritance or luck. One does need the exact DNA to keep money; otherwise, the situation will be like a lot of lottery winners or in the case of Ben Gunn in Treasure Island, frittering away a significant amount and back to the normal life.

READING PASSAGE 3

You should spend about 20 minutes on **Questions 28-40**, which are based on Reading Passage 3 below.

Business School Cases:
What Else Do You Still Need to Know About Money

A. "All of us had an ample share of the treasure and used it wisely or foolishly, according to our natures." "Captain Smollett is now retired from the sea. Gray not only saved his money, but being suddenly smit with the desire to rise, also studied his profession, and he is now mate and part owner of a fine-rigged ship, married besides, and the father of a family. As for Ben Gunn, he got a thousand pounds, which he spent or lost in three weeks, or to be more exact, in nineteen days."

B. These quotes have been closely linked to one's spending habits and use of money. These also correspond to several notions mentioning in one of the bestsellers, *The Wealth Elite*. It is not about the inheritance or luck. One does need the exact DNA to keep money; otherwise, the situation will be like a lot of lottery winners or in the case of *Ben Gunn* in *Treasure Island*, frittering away a significant amount and back to the normal life.

C. It is the chance event and other factors that lead to the discovery of gold on Treasure Island, and three main characters have been a summarized version of all people. There are some who like Gray knowing the importance of stashing money and at the same time he tries to cultivate his profession so that more knowledge and seasoned skills will bring him more salaries at work. There are others who simply retire and live a simple life like Captain Smollet.

D. In other classics, a similar idea can also be found. In *The 30,000 Bequest*, a famous tale from Mark Twain, one of the main characters, Electra, clearly has the millionaire mindsets even though she is only 19. She uses her savings to buy an acre of land. Then she manages to save more money and uses the money and the passive income to multiply her fortune, whereas in another classic, *The 1,000,000 Bank Note*, Henry does not have the rich DNA. But just like Ben Gunn, he is a lucky person who gets the 1,000,000 Bank Note. Otherwise, he will just be a broker who does not seem as aggressive as Electra, and will not use other strategies to get more wealth. It remains inconclusive to know whether Henry will keep the fortune he gets or whether he is going to end up like Ben Gunn.

E. Other than cultivating or knowing the rich DNA, one truly needs to know one's passion, a key golden rule from one of the bestsellers, *Homeless to Billionaire*. This shares a similar vein to the concept from *Where You Go Is Not Who You Will Be*. If you do not know what you love, chances are that you won't be making a lot of money. If you love what you do, the career can be lasting. One's high salary rests on accumulated job experiences in a specific domain. The meticulously honed skills will earn you more money, while the person who constantly changes the job gets a mediocre salary.

F. In *Homeless to Billionaire*, the author further informs us that "not being able to recognize your passion can be a problem for those who stuck in jobs that they do not enjoy." If work has become a routine, it makes you resent the job or feel listless at work, making you highly unlikely to reach the goal or have a great job performance.

G. The author has offered us some good ways to find our passion. Suggestions like, what could you do for five years straight without getting paid? It is actually a good way. When you have found the true passion, you will notice that everything has changed. Even if you do not make as much as you used to, you feel fulfilled. Your passion will make your career sustained, leading to higher salary in the long-term. You won't feel you are like the author of *The Promise of a Pencil*. The name of a renowned company and seemingly glamourous life cannot seem to cover the inner voice inside him.

H. When happiness is ebbing, the red flag inside you will be increasingly prominent. Money won't mean anything, unless there is a meaning in the job. Striking a balance between life choices has not always been easy. However, with the right mindset and passion, you will surely be the kind of the person you want to be. You will see the rainbow each day even if it is just a normal day. Appreciate the present moment, and you will eventually get the result you have been hoping for, even wealth.

Questions 28-31
Complete each sentence with the correct ending, A-H below.
Write the correct letter, A-H, in boxes 28-31 on your answer
sheet.

28 To retain money, one needs to possess

29 To get more payment, one needs to have

30 To make lots of currency, one needs to have

31 To procreate more wealth, one needs to have

A the bestowal of wealth from parents
B the random chance to find the treasure
C the acquaintance from higher-ups
D the distinctive qualities
E the passion for one's work
F the education in a specific domain
G the dormant earnings
H the weak ties

Test 1

1
TEST
Reading Passage 3

2
TEST

3
TEST

4
TEST

Questions 32-38

Look at the following statements (Questions 32-38) and the list of books below.

Match each statement with the correct book, A-G

Write the correct letter, A-G, in boxes 32-38 on your answer sheet.

NB You may use any letter more than once.

32 superficial stuff cannot fill the void inside one's body

33 occupation development is highly relevant to one's drive

34 inborn traits will decide one's ability to collect wealth

35 innate characteristics will determine one's use of treasure

36 detection of what you love is the way to get out of the dilemma

37 one's wealth is primarily due to a serendipitous encounter

38 one's wealth is primarily due to financial quotient

List of books

A *Homeless to Billionaire*

B *The 1,000,000 Bank Note*

C *Where You Go Is Not Who You Will Be*

D *The Wealth Elite*

E *Treasure Island*

F *The 30,000 Bequest*

G *The Promise of a Pencil*

Questions 39-40

Do the following statements agree with the information given in the Reading Passage 3

In boxes 39-40 on your answer sheet, write

> **TRUE**- if the statement agrees with the information
> **FALSE**- if the statement contradicts the information
> **NOT GIVEN**- if there is no information on this

39. Henry is bound to be more wealthy than Electra because he already has the 1,000,000 Bank Note.

40. With the right mindset and appreciation, one is capable of getting things, including wealth.

解析

03 ｜英國文學＋商管

《*Treasure Island*》、《*The Wealth Elite*》、《*Homeless to Billionaire*》和《*The Secrets of Getting Rich*》
關於金錢你還需要知道些什麼呢？

在答題前第一個步驟是先快速掃視題目題型並快速制定答題策略，在這篇很快可以看到配對完成句子題＋配對題＋判斷題，這篇的難度算是 test 1 中最難的一篇，採取順答策略，並且同步答配對題＋判斷題，最後答完成句子題，時間才夠。

◆ 很快看到第一段有關於金銀島中三個人物在金錢使用上的不同，這發生於獲取金銀島的寶藏之後。接續看到第二段第一句 These quotes have been closely linked to one's spending habits and use of money. These also correspond to several notions mentioning in one of the bestsellers, *The Wealth Elite*.，可以先在 32-38 題的敘述中找相對應的點。接續讀到 It is not about the inheritance or luck. One does need the exact DNA to keep money，可以對應到第 34 題的敘述 inborn traits will decide one's ability to collect wealth，天生的特質即 DNA 才是決定一個人 collect wealth 的關鍵，不然就會像 Ben Gunn 那樣揮霍光，**第 34 題答案為 D**。

◆ 接著讀到第四段的部分，*The 30,000 Bequest*，從中可以得知伊萊克特顯然就具備了百萬富翁的心態，即使她才年僅 19 歲。她接著設法存下更多的錢並且使用錢和被動收入讓自己的財富數倍成長，反推出她具有 financial quotient，對應到題目的 one's wealth is primarily due to financial quotient，故第 38 題答案要選 **F**。

- 接續讀到 *The 1,000,000 Bank Note*，Henry does not have the rich DNA. But just like Ben Gunn, he is a lucky person who gets the 1,000,000 Bank Note.，他是幸運得到一筆錢，這點可以對應到**第 37 題**的 one's wealth is primarily due to a serendipitous encounter，故答案要選 **B**。

- 接著讀完這個段落順便答判斷題第 39 題的部分，Henry is bound to be more wealthy than Electra because he already has the 1,000,000 Bank Note，但是段落敘述中僅分別提到兩個人，但是並敘述兩人之間誰會獲取更多的錢，故答案要選 NOT GIVEN，在雅思閱讀的判斷題中很常有這樣的考點，兩者之間沒有比較的話**要選 NOT GIVEN**。

- 接續讀第 5 段，Other than cultivating or knowing the rich DNA, one truly needs to know one's passion, a key golden rule from one of the bestsellers, ***Homeless to Billionaire***. This shares a similar vein to the concept from ***Where You Go Is Not Who You Will Be***. If you do not know what you love, chances are that you won't be making a lot of money. If you love what you do, the career can be lasting. One's high salary rests on accumulated job experiences in a specific domain. The meticulously honed skills will earn you more money, while the person who constantly changes the job gets a mediocre salary. ，當中提到了兩本書，所以很可能都是考點，One's high salary rests on accumulated job experiences in a specific domain.對應到 occupation development is highly relevant to one's drive，故第 **33** 題要選 **C**。

♦ 接續讀到下一段，In *Homeless to Billionaire*, the author further informs us that "not being able to recognize your passion can be a problem for those stuck in jobs that they do not enjoy."，當中的 stuck in jobs 對應到 dilemma，也就是第 36 題的描述 detection of what you love is the way to get out of the dilemma，而 recognize 對應到 **detection**，故第 **36** 題要選 **A**。

♦ 接續讀到 You won't feel you are like the author of *The Promise of a Pencil*. The name of a renowned company and seemingly glamourous life cannot seem to cover the inner voice inside him. ，可以對應到**第 32 題**的 superficial stuff cannot fill the void inside one's body，光鮮的生活和頭銜等沒辦法填補內心的空虛，故答案要選 **G**。

◆ 接著看完最後一段，並在最後一句 Appreciate the present moment, and you will eventually get the result you have been hoping for, even wealth.找到判斷題**第 40 題**的對應處，且描述和題目敘述吻合，**故答案要選 True**。

◆ 最後來答配對題完成句子題，真的比較不好答的題型，先從第 28 題開始 To retain money, one needs to possess... ，retain money 可以對應到 keep money，即 It is not about the inheritance or luck. One does need the exact DNA to keep money，所以是要有特定的特質才能將錢守住，**答案要選 D**，the distinctive qualities。

◆ 再來看**第 29 題**，To get more payment, one needs to have，more payment 要對應到 There are some who like Gray knowing the importance of stashing money and at the same time he tries to cultivate his profession so that more knowledge and seasoned skills will bring him **more salaries** at work.，藉由在自己領域的耕耘，累積更專業的技能後就能獲取更多的薪資 more salaries，故答案要選 the education in a specific domain，**即 F**，當中 education 對應到 **knowledge**。

◆ 再來看**第 30 題**，To make lots of currency, one needs to have... ，對應到 If you do not know what you love, chances

Test 1

1 Reading Passage 3

TEST 1

TEST 2

TEST 3

TEST 4

are that you won't be **making a lot of money**. If you love what you do, the career can be lasting. One's high salary rests on accumulated job experiences in a specific domain.，**the passion for one's work**，即 **E**。Make a lot of money 對應到 make lots of currency 且這題談到的是工作熱情和賺錢之間的關聯性，跟 Gray 的部分不太同，Gray 的部分僅是知道要這麼做，並持續耕耘，但是並未提到兩者間的關聯性。藉由熱情讓事業持續後才能賺大錢，跟單純獲取高薪資不同。

◆ **第 31 題**，To procreate more wealth, one needs to have...，procreate 指的是製造和增生，**要選 G**，the dormant earnings，這點可以對應到 one of the main characters, Electra, clearly has the millionaire mindsets even though she is only 19. She uses her savings to buy an acre of land. Then she manages to save more money and uses the money and the passive income to multiplies her fortune 中的 multiplies her fortune，當中 passive 對應到 **dormant**。

"All of us had an **1.**_____ share of the treasure and used it wisely or foolishly, according to our **2.**_____." "Captain Smollett is now retired from the sea. Gray not only saved his money, but being suddenly smit with the **3.**_____ to rise, also studied his **4.**_____, and he is now mate and part owner of a fine-rigged ship, married besides, and the father of a family. As for Ben Gunn, he got a thousand pounds, which he spent or lost in three weeks, or to be more exact, in nineteen days."

...These also correspond to several **5.**_____ mentioning in one of the bestsellers, *The Wealth Elite*. It is not about the **6.**_____ or luck. One does need the exact DNA to keep money; otherwise, the situation will be like a lot of lottery winners or in the case of *Ben Gunn* in *Treasure Island*, frittering away a significant amount and back to the **7.**_____ life.

It is the chance event and other factors that lead to the discovery of gold on Treasure Island, and three main characters have been a **8.**_____ version of all people. There are some who like Gray knowing the importance of **9.**_____ money and at the same time he tries to **10.**_____ his profession so that more knowledge and **11.**_____ skills will bring him more salaries at work. There are others who simply retire and live a simple life like Captain Smollet.

...In *The 30,000 Bequest*, a famous tale from Mark Twain, one of the main characters, Electra, clearly has the millionaire mindsets even though she is only 19. She uses her savings to buy an **12.** ___ _____ of land. Then she manages to save more money and uses the money and the **13.** _____ income to multiply her **14.** _____, whereas in another classic, *The 1,000,000 Bank Note*, Henry does not have the rich DNA...Otherwise, he will just be a broker who does not seem as **15.** _____ as Electra, and will not use other strategies to get more **16.** _____....

Other than cultivating or knowing the rich DNA, one truly needs to know one's **17.** _____, a key golden rule from one of the bestsellers, *Homeless to Billionaire*. This shares a similar vein to the concept from *Where You Go Is Not Who You Will Be*. If you do not know what you love, **18.** _____ are that you won't be making a lot of money. If you love what you do, the career can be lasting. One's high **19.** _____ rests on accumulated job experiences in a specific **20.** _____. The meticulously **21.** ___ _____ skills will earn you more money, while the person who constantly changes the job gets a **22.** _____ salary.

In *Homeless to Billionaire*, the author further informs us that "not being able to **23.** _____ your passion can be a problem for those who stuck in jobs that they do not enjoy." If work has become a **24.** _____, it makes you **25.** _____ ___ the job or feel listless at work, making you highly unlikely to reach the goal or have a great job **26.** _____.

...When you have found the true passion, you will notice that everything has changed. Even if you do not make as much as you used to, you feel fulfilled. Your passion will make your career **27.** _____, leading to higher salary in the long-term. You won't feel you are like the author of *The Promise of a Pencil*. The name of a **28.**_____ company and seemingly **29.**_____ life cannot seem to cover the inner **30.**_____ inside him.

When happiness is ebbing, the red flag inside you will be increasingly **31.**_____. Money won't mean anything, unless there is a meaning in the job. Striking a balance between life choices has not always been easy. However, with the right **32.**_____ and passion, you will surely be the kind of the person you want to be. You will see the rainbow each day even if it is just a normal day. Appreciate the present moment, and you will eventually get the result you have been hoping for, even wealth.

中譯和影子跟讀　　　　　🔊 MP3 015

A. "All of us had an ample share of the treasure and used it wisely or foolishly, according to our natures." "Captain Smollett is now retired from the sea. Gray not only saved his money, but being suddenly smit with the desire to rise, also studied his profession, and he is now mate and part owner of a fine-rigged ship, married besides, and the father of a family. As for Ben Gunn, he got a thousand pounds, which he spent or lost in three weeks, or to be more exact, in nineteen days."

「我們每個人都分得足額份的寶藏，而在寶藏的運用上是明智地或欠缺考量，這點全憑天性而定」。「史莫列特船長現從航海生活中退休了」。「格雷不僅存到錢，且突然有著進取心，深耕自己的專業能力，他現在是艘裝備齊全的大副與股東，還結了婚，當了父親。至於班・剛恩，將分得的一千英鎊於三週內就揮霍光，或是更確切地說，十九天就將錢用光了」。

B. These quotes have been closely linked to one's spending habits and use of money. These also correspond to several notions mentioning in one of the bestsellers, *The Wealth Elite*. It is not about the inheritance or luck. One does need the exact DNA to keep money; otherwise, the situation will be like a lot of lottery winners or in the case of *Ben Gunn* in *Treasure Island*, frittering away a significant amount and back to the normal life.

這些引述句都與一個人花費習慣和金錢的使用有關連。這些也與其中一本暢銷書《財富菁英》，所提到的幾個觀念有所吻合。並不是取決於遺產或幸運。一個人需要確切的 DNA 以留住金錢，否則，情況就會像是許多樂透贏家或是在《金銀島》案例中所提到的班·剛恩一樣，揮霍掉大量的錢，又回到本來普通的生活。

C. It is the chance event and other factors that lead to the discovery of gold on Treasure Island, and three main characters have been a summarized version of all people. There are some who like Gray knowing the importance of stashing money and at the same time he tries to cultivate his profession so that more knowledge and seasoned skills will bring him more salaries at work. There are others who simply retire and live a simple life like Captain Smollet.

是機運和其他因素促成在金銀島上發現黃金，而三位主角恰巧一直是大眾的摘要版本。有些人會像格雷一樣，懂得金錢儲蓄的重要性，與此同時他又試圖耕植自己的專業領域，如此一來，更多的知識和專業技能會替他在工作中贏得更多的薪資。還有其他人就是單純選擇退休且過著像史莫列特船長那樣簡樸的生活。

D. In other classics, a similar idea can also be found. In *The 30,000 Bequest*, a famous tale from Mark Twain, one of the main characters, Electra, clearly has the millionaire mindsets even though she is only 19. She uses her savings to buy an acre of land. Then she manages to save more money and uses the money and the passive income to multiplies her fortune, whereas in another classic, *The 1,000,000 Bank Note*, Henry does not have the rich DNA. But just like Ben Gunn, he is a lucky person who gets the 1,000,000 Bank Note. Otherwise, he will just be a broker who does not seem as aggressive as Electra, and will not use other strategies to get more wealth. It remains inconclusive to know whether Henry will keep the fortune he gets or whether he is going to end up like Ben Gunn.

在其他經典鉅作中，也能察覺出相似的觀點。在《三萬美元遺產》，馬克·吐溫的一則名故事中，其中一位主要的角色，伊萊克特顯然就具備了百萬富翁的心態，即使她才年僅 19 歲。她用存款買了一英畝的地，接著設法存下更多的錢並且使用錢和被動收入讓自己的財富數倍成長，反之，在《百萬英鎊》裡，亨利不具備有錢人的 DNA。但就像是班·剛恩一樣，他是個得到百萬英鎊的幸運小夥子。否則，他就僅是位股票經紀人，似乎沒有伊萊克特那樣的進取心，且不會運用其他策略以獲得更多的財富。亨利是否能持續利用財富以得到自己想要的或是他會否像班·剛恩的下場一樣，關於這點是無法下定論的。

E. Other than cultivating or knowing the rich DNA, one truly needs to know one's passion, a key golden rule from one of the bestsellers, *Homeless to Billionaire*. This shares a similar vein to the concept from *Where You Go Is Not Who You Will Be*. If you do not know what you love, chances are that you won't be making a lot of money. If you love what you do, the career can be lasting. One's high salary rests on accumulated job experiences in a specific domain. The meticulously honed skills will earn you more money, while the person who constantly changes the job gets a mediocre salary.

除了培養或了解財富 DNA，一個人真的需要了解自我的熱情，其中一本暢銷書《無家可歸到十億富翁》的關鍵黃金定律。這個觀點也與《你讀的學校無法決定你能成為什麼樣的人》如出一轍。如果你不知道你自己的愛好，很可能你沒辦法賺取許多錢。如果你喜愛你所從事的，職涯是能夠持久下去的。一個人的高薪是基於在一個特定領域中累積工作經驗

Test 1

TEST 1
Reading Passage 3

TEST 2

TEST 3

TEST 4

而得。一絲不苟地鍛鍊出的技能會為你帶來更多的錢，而常換工作者得到平庸的薪資。

F. In *Homeless to Billionaire*, the author further informs us that "not being able to recognize your passion can be a problem for those who stuck in jobs that they do not enjoy." If work has become a routine, it makes you resent the job or feel listless at work, making you highly unlikely to reach the goal or have a great job performance.

在《無家可歸到十億富翁》，作者更進一步告知我們「對於那些在工作上無法樂在其中的人來說，無法辨識出你的熱情會成為你的問題，而使你裹足不前」。如果工作已經成了例行公事，會讓你怨恨這份工作或是在工作時覺得無精打采，讓你更難達到目標或是有更好的工作表現。

G. The author has offered us some good ways to find our passion. Suggestions like, what could you do for five years straight without getting paid? It is actually a good way. When you have found the true passion, you will notice that everything has changed. Even if you do not make as much as you used to, you feel fulfilled. Your passion will make your career sustained, leading to higher salary in the long-term. You won't feel you are like the author of *The Promise of a Pencil*. The name of a renowned company and seemingly glamourous life cannot seem to cover the inner voice inside him.

對此，作者也提供了一些好的方法讓我們找到自己的熱情。當中的建議像是，什麼事情是你可以不支薪但卻能夠連續五年都從事的呢？這實際上是個好方法。當你已經找到真正的熱情時，你將發現事情有所改變了。即使你賺取的沒有像往常那麼多，你會感到踏實。你的熱情會讓你的職涯持續下去，在後期獲取更高的薪資。你不會像是《一枝鉛筆的承諾》的作者那樣。享譽盛名的公司名稱和看起來光鮮的生活似乎無法蓋過在他內心的聲音。

H. When happiness is ebbing, the red flag inside you will be increasingly prominent. Money won't mean anything, unless there is a meaning in the job. Striking a balance between life choices has not always been easy. However, with the right mindset and passion, you will surely be the kind of the person you want to be. You will see the rainbow each day even if it is just a normal day. Appreciate the present moment, and you will eventually get the result you have been hoping for, even wealth.

當幸福感消逝時，你心裡的紅旗就會日益地顯著。金錢並不能代表任何事情，除非在那份工作上頭有意義存在。在人生的選擇上取得平衡一直都不是那麼容易。然而，有著正確的心態和熱情，你確實會成為你想要成為的那個人。你將會每天都看到彩虹，即使那僅是個再普通不過的一天。感謝現在這個時刻，而你終將得到你一直都期盼的結果，甚至是財富。

參考答案

Test 1

Reading passage 1 (1-13)

1. D
2. A
3. D
4. C
5. B
6. D
7. C
8. G
9. F
10. interpreter
11. producer
12. recruiter
13. memorizing

Reading passage 2 (14-27)

14. pectoral fin
15. pelvic fin
16. dorsal fin
17. adipose fin
18. anal fin
19. caudal fin
20. adipose
21. vacillate
22. sperm
23. stupefied
24. False
25. Not Given
26. True
27. True

Reading passage 3 (28-40)

28. D
29. F
30. E
31. G
32. G
33. C
34. D
35. E
36. A
37. B
38. F
39. Not Given
40. True

聽讀整合 參考答案

Test 1 P1

1. pivotal
2. resumes
3. whimsical
4. random
5. unexpectedly
6. lucrative
7. statement
8. console
9. assistant
10. position
11. static
12. promoted
13. performance
14. editor
15. opportunities
16. existing
17. believer
18. smooth
19. attempts
20. executive
21. advertising
22. accumulated
23. outcome
24. windshield
25. recruiter
26. rejection
27. preparation
28. algorithms
29. memorizing
30. hypothetical
31. perseverance
32. interpreter

Test 1 P2

1. punished
2. yacht
3. kindheartedness
4. witnesses
5. bystanders
6. recovered
7. mermaid
8. serendipitous
9. wriggling
10. pearl
11. incarnation
12. biology
13. anatomy
14. nuisance
15. unexpected
16. accolades

17. reliant
18. oxygen
19. gill
20. analogous
21. maneuverability
22. stability
23. puzzle
24. sense
25. pressure
26. undulations
27. delivery
28. stupefying
29. hidden
30. venom
31. distinctive
32. flair

Test 1 P3

1. ample
2. natures
3. desire
4. profession
5. notions
6. inheritance
7. normal
8. summarized
9. stashing
10. cultivate
11. seasoned
12. acre
13. passive
14. fortune
15. aggressive
16. wealth
17. passion
18. chances
19. salary
20. domain
21. honed
22. mediocre
23. recognize
24. routine
25. resent
26. performance
27. sustained
28. renowned
29. glamourous
30. voice
31. prominent
32. mindset

Test 2

篇章概述

04

在各家電視台競爭激烈、百家爭鳴的情況下，要如何脫穎而出呢？

在這篇很快可以看到配對題的部分，配對題大多是依順序出題，所以採取「順答」，照文章段落順序閱讀文章並答題。這篇也是相對好答的題目，只是要注意摘要題的有些答案是需要根據空格的語法去調整答案。

05

船長為何願意放棄一切並把豐碩的物資交給西爾佛和他的黨羽呢？

這篇中有四個題型，加上有完成句子配對題所以較難答，是目前難度較高的一篇試題。

06

人生的酸甜苦辣和如何面對逆境和挫折

在這篇很快可以看到配對題和段落細節題，不過段落細節題有時候蠻隱晦不太好答，可以快速掃描並記憶相關關鍵字，邊閱讀邊答。

 **Test 2**

READING PASSAGE 1

You should spend about 20 minutes on **Questions 1-13**, which are based on Reading Passage 1 below.

Business School Cases: How to Stand out from the Crowd

A. In *Getting There*, CBS president and CEO, Leslie Moonves once said "some shows end up being hits, but two out of three fail." and "we get pitched about five hundred television shows a year and only put four new ones on the air." Form these statements, a conclusion can be drawn about fierce competition among different networks and producers. Each season is made up of 10 to 23 episodes with only a tight budget and some shows are truly expensive to make. If a show gets to last to four seasons, it is considered a pretty popular show.

B. Since the ending of one season requires the network to continually be willing to finance or support the show or outside investors are acknowledging the potential and thus want to keep pouring money into the show. Otherwise, the show goes dead. At another instance, fans begging for the show to be back sometimes will work.

C. Good ratings are the guarantee for the show to last, especially the first few episodes. Some shows are ruthlessly killed and are getting replaced by a back-up, if the first few episodes are not popular. How to attract audiences in the first few episodes is the key, and research in the success of the show has included two successful shows that adopt the same strategy to make the show appealing. The two shows include *Damages* and *Suits*. Both are cliffhangers in the very first episode that consists of the interview scenes. Since everyone has to go to the interview throughout their whole life, audiences want to know how to nail the interview. What makes them glued to the set or Netflix is the riveting scene in which the outcome of the interview cannot be predicted.

D. In *Damages*, Ellen Parsons is an outstanding law graduate who goes on an interview at Hollis Nye's law firm, and after the chat, the firm is ready to discuss further details and benefits with Ellen, but is shocked by the fact that Ellen is eyeing another prestigious law firm, Hewes & Associates. But Hewes & Associates, based on its reputation, can have anyone whether it is a seasoned senior lawyer or a newly graduate whose ability is better than Ellen. Yet Ellen goes to the scheduled interview where she meets affable Tom, who is the friend of Patty and a senior partner of the company. Tom is cordial and candid, unlike other interviews who will employ different interview strategies during the interview. He even gives the advice to Ellen to help her better prepare for the ultimate interview with the boss, Patty. Things go well until Tom announces the time of the scheduled interview, which is on Saturday. Ellen is astounded to hear the date because her sister's wedding is on the same date. How to choose between a lucrative job that everyone is dying to get in and attending her sister's wedding is what allures audiences to continue watching till the end of the first episode.

E. In *Suits*, the first episode of the show consists of several great blends that will get your adrenaline rush going. It starts with the main character Mike Ross illegitimately taking LSAT for others, and he is almost getting caught. But his agility in changing the outfit saves him in the situation. His desperation for money to pay for his grandmother's health expenses leads to his misdemeanor of illegal transporting the marijuana for his friend, Trevor.

F. At the hotel, his observation for each location and signs saves him from getting arrested by the policemen. "Gloves", "The pool is closed", and "the Harvard law interview event" are the key. When he heads toward the scheduled room, he sees two guys outside the room, who obviously are not the waiter and the guest. He verifies their identities by asking questions on what he sees beforehand. Then both sides soon figure each other out, and that leads to a chase. Then he rushes downstairs and heads to the event. There he gets asked a question by the gatekeeper interviewer. She will ask a question and give a facial expression to the interviewer on whether the person is qualified or not. Mike is confronted with the question of "You are five minutes late. Is there a reason that I should let you in". To which, he replies "I'm just trying to ditch the cop. I don't care if you let me in or not." The action earns him the first nod from the female gatekeeper. And there are other great scenarios that will certainly keep audiences intrigued, such as how to get hired by the law firm without a Harvard degree.

Questions 1-4

Choose the correct letter, A, B, C, or D

Write the correct letter in boxes 1-4 on your answer sheet

1. In the first paragraph, the conclusion about the fierce competition among producers and networks has been based on?
   A. the length has to last to 4 seasons.
   B. the percentage
   C. the tight budget
   D. the tight deadline

2. In the second and third paragraph, what can be inferred about a show that is not a hit?
   A. it gets retained
   B. it will generate good ratings in the long term
   C. it will be bound to be saved by fans
   D. it will be abandoned

3. In the third paragraph, how to make the show appealing?
   A. by interviewing great actors and actresses
   B. by predicting the outcome of the interview
   C. by adopting the interview suggestions
   D. by including new elements that are gripping

4. In the fourth paragraph, what can be inferred about the interview at Hewes & Associates?

A. Tom has mentioned about benefits and payment.

B. Tom is a difficult interviewer.

C. Tom offers some tips to Ellen

D. Tom is not pleased to hear the news of Ellen's wedding.

Questions 5-13

Complete the notes below

Choose ONE WORD ONLY from the passage for each answer

Write your answers in boxes 5-13 on your answer sheet.

	EVENTS
Damages	● Hewes & Associates, based on its reputation can hire lawyers with **5.**_____ or better capability.
	● Tom's **6.**_____ at the scheduled interview has marked a great beginning.
	● Eventually, Ellen has a **7.**_____ schedule for the next interview because her sister's wedding is on the same date.
	● Making the choose between a **8.**_____ job that and attending her sister's wedding is what keeps the audiences loyal.

Suits	● In *Suits*, **9.**_____ of taking LSAT for others almost makes Mike getting caught, but outfit changes save him in the situation.
	● His desperation for money has led to his willingness of **10.**_____ transporting the marijuana for his friend, Trevor.
	● At the hotel, his observation for each location and signs saves him from getting arrested by the policemen.
	● Before the chase, he verifies the **11.**_____ of the two guys by asking his observations. These include the event of Harvard law interview and the **12.**_____ of the pool.
	● "I'm just trying to ditch the cop. I don't care if you let me in or not." is what makes Mike get the **13.**_____ from the female interviewer.

04 ｜商管＋面試＋法律

《*Getting There*》、《金權遊戲》、《金裝律師》

在各家電視台競爭激烈、百家爭鳴的情況下，要如何脫穎而出呢？

在答題前第一個步驟是先快速掃視題目題型並快速制定答題策略，在這篇很快可以看到配對題的部分，配對題大多是依順序出題，所以採取「**順答**」，照文章段落順序閱讀文章並答題。這篇也是相對好答的題目，只是要注意摘要題的有些答案是需要根據空格的語法去調整答案。

◆ **第 1 題**，in the first paragraph, the conclusion about the fierce competition among producers and networks has been based on，要注意題目問的是競爭的部分而非流行度，故要排除 A 的 the length has to last to 4 seasons。**B 選項的 percentage 為正確答案**，關於這部分可以定位到 In *Getting There*, CBS president and CEO, Leslie Moonves once said "some shows end up being hits, but two out of three fail." and "we get pitched about five hundred television shows a year and only put four new ones on the air."，對電視台來説成功率只有 1/3，而對那些推銷節目的製作人來説是 500 選 4，所以競爭是很激烈的。

◆ **第 2 題**，in the second and third paragraph, what can be

inferred about a show that is not a hit 中，A，it gets retained，不是 hit 的話，節目就會被砍掉，故要排除 A。B，it will generate the good ratings in the long term，或許有可能，但是對電視台高層來說，不可能有時間等你，只會像段落敘述中的 Some shows are ruthlessly killed and are getting replaced by a back-up, if the first few episodes are not popular.，故也可以排除 B。C，it will be bound to be saved by fans，這點在第二段結尾有提到，不過機率太低了，正常情況下還是被砍掉了，故要排除 C。D，it will be abandoned，此為正確答案，故**要選 D**。

◆ **第 3 題**，In the third paragraph, how to make the show appealing? A，by interviewing great actors and actresses，跟面試演員的部分無關，僅提到採用面試的情節吸引人，故要排除 A。B，by predicting the outcome of the interview，也跟推測面試結果無關，故要排除 B。C，by adopting the interview suggestions，跟面試採用的建議也無關，故要排除 C。D，by including new elements that are gripping，new elements 可以理解成廣義的 interview 的代稱，加入新元素/加入新的面試元素，且是引人入勝的，故**答案要選 D**。

◆ **第 4 題**，in the fourth paragraph, what can be inferred about the interview at Hewes & Associates?，A，Tom has mentioned about benefits and payment.，Tom 沒有提到，反而是另一間公司有提到，故要排除 A。B，Tom is a difficult interviewer.，但原文敘述中 Tom is cordial and candid，故要排除 B。C，Tom offers some tips to Ellen，Tom 有提供她建議，故要選 C。D，Tom is not pleased to hear the news of Ellen's wedding.，段落中並沒有這樣的陳述，故要排除 D。

◆ **第 5 題**，Hewes & Associates, based on its reputation can hire lawyers with **5.**＿＿＿＿＿ or better capability.，這部分可以對應到 But Hewes & Associates, based on its reputation, can have anyone whether it is a seasoned senior lawyer or a newly graduate whose ability is better than Ellen.，**better capability** 對應到 whose ability is better than，所以空格處要對應到 or 前面的敘述部分，並藉由 seasoned 推斷出要有經驗的，故答案要填 **experience**。這題稍難。

◆ **第 6 題**，Tom's **6.**＿＿＿＿＿ at the scheduled interview has marked a great beginning.這部分對應到 Yet Ellen goes to the scheduled interview where she meets **affable** Tom, who is the friend of Patty and a senior partner of the company.，空格要填 affable 的名詞，故要改成 **affability**。

◆ **第 7 題**，Eventually, Ellen has a **7.**＿＿＿＿＿ schedule for the next interview because her sister's wedding is on the same date.這部分對應到 Ellen is astounded to hear the date because her sister's wedding is on the same date. How to choose between a lucrative job that everyone is dying to get in and attending her sister's wedding is what allures audiences to continue watching till the end of the first episode.所以可以反推出 Ellen 跟下次面試的時程是 conflicting 的,**答案要選 conflicting**。

◆ **第 8 題**,Making the choose between a **8.**＿＿＿＿＿ job that everyone is dying to get in and attending her sister's wedding is what keeps the audiences loyal. 這部分對應到 How to choose between a lucrative job that everyone is dying to get in and attending her sister's wedding is what allures audiences to continue watching till the end of the first episode.這題很簡單,直接對應到 lucrative,故**答案是 lucrative**。

◆ **第 9 題**,In *Suits*, **9.**＿＿＿＿＿ of taking LSAT for others almost makes Mike getting caught, but outfit changes save him in the situation. 這部分對應到 It starts with the main character Milk Ross illegitimately taking LSAT for others, and he is almost getting caught.空格對應到 illegitimately,但根據語法要改成 illegitimacy 才對,故**答案為 illegitimacy**。

◆ **第 10 題**,His desperation for money has led to his

willingness of **10.**＿＿＿＿ transporting the marijuana for his friend, Trevor. 這部分對應到 His desperate for money to pay for his grandmother's health expenses leads to his misdemeanor of illegal transporting the marijuana for his friend, Trevor.空格處對應到 illegal，但要改成副詞才合乎語法，故答案為 **illegally**。

◆ **第 11 題**，At the hotel, his observation for each location and signs saves him from getting arrested by the policemen. Before the chase, he verifies the **11.**＿＿＿＿ of the two guys by asking his observations. 這部分對應到 He verifies their identities by asking questions on what he sees beforehand.，故答案為 **identities**。

◆ **第 12 題**，These include the event of Harvard law interview and the **12.**＿＿＿＿ of the pool. 這部分對應到 At the hotel, his observation for each location and signs saves him from getting arrest by the policemen. "Gloves", "The pool is closed", and "the Harvard law interview event" are the key.，空格處對應到 closed，但要改成名詞才合乎語法，故答案為 **closure**。

◆ **第 13 題**，"I'm just trying to ditch the cop. I don't care if you let me in or not." is what makes Mike get the **13.**＿＿＿＿

___ from the female interviewer. 這部分對應到 Is there a reason that I should let you in". To which, he replies "I'm just trying to ditch the cop. I don't care if you let me in or not." The action earns him the first **nod** from the female gatekeeper. ,答案很明顯是 **nod**。

In *Getting There*, CBS **1.**_____ and CEO, Leslie Moonves once said "some shows end up being hits, but two out of three fail." and "we get **2.**_____ about five hundred **3.**_____ __ shows a year and only put four new ones on the air." Form these statements, a conclusion can be drawn about fierce **4.**___ _____ among different networks and **5.**_____. Each season is made up of 10 to 23 **6.**_____ with only a tight budget and some shows are truly **7.**_____ to make. If a show gets to last to four seasons, it is considered a pretty popular show.

Since the ending of one season requires the network to continually be willing to finance or **8.**_____ the show or outside investors are **9.**_____ the potential and thus want to keep **10.**_____ money into the show...

Good ratings are the **11.**_____ for the show to last, especially the first few episodes. Some shows are **12.**_____ __ killed and are getting replaced by a back-up, if the first few episodes are not popular. How to attract **13.**_____ in the first few episodes is the key, and research in the success of the show has included two successful shows that **14.**_____ the same strategy to make the show **15.**_____. The two shows include *Damages* and *Suits*. Both are **16.**_____ in the very first episode that consists of the interview scenes. Since everyone has to go to the interview throughout their whole life, audiences want to know how to **17.**_____ the interview.

What makes them glued to the set or Netflix is the riveting scene in which the **18.**_____ of the interview cannot be predicted.

In *Damages*, Ellen Parsons is an outstanding law graduate who goes on an interview at Hollis Nye's law firm, and after the chat, the firm is ready to discuss further details and **19.**_____ with Ellen, but is shocked by the fact that Ellen is eyeing another **20.**_____ law firm, Hewes & Associates. But Hewes & Associates, based on its **21.**_____, can have anyone whether it is a **22.**_____ senior lawyer or a newly graduate whose ability is better than Ellen. Yet Ellen goes to the **23.**_____ interview where she meets **24.**_____ Tom, who is the friend of Patty and a senior partner of the company. Tom is **25.**_____ and candid, unlike other interviews who will **26.**_____ different interview strategies during the interview. He even gives the advice to Ellen to help her better prepare for the **27.**_____ interview with the boss, Patty. Things go well until Tom announces the time of the scheduled interview, which is on **28.**_____. Ellen is astounded to hear the date because her sister's wedding is on the same date....

In *Suits*, the first episode of the show consists of several great blends that will get your adrenaline rush going. It starts with the main character Mike Ross **29.**_____ taking LSAT for others, and he is almost getting caught. But his agility in changing the outfit saves him in the situation. His desperation for money to pay for his grandmother's health expenses leads to his **30.**_____ of illegal transporting the marijuana for his friend, Trevor.

At the hotel, his observation for each location and signs saves him from getting arrested by the policemen. "Gloves", "The pool is closed", and "the Harvard law interview event" are the key. When he heads toward the scheduled room, he sees two guys outside the room, who obviously are not the waiter and the guest. He verifies their **31.**_____ by asking questions on what he sees beforehand. Then both sides soon figure each other out, and that leads to a chase. Then he rushes **32.**_____

_____ and heads to the event. There he gets asked a question by the gatekeeper interviewer. She will ask a question and give a facial expression to the interviewer on whether the person is qualified or not. Mike is confronted with the question of "You are five minutes late. Is there a reason that I should let you in". To which, he replies "I'm just trying to ditch the cop. I don't care if you let me in or not." The action earns him the first nod from the female gatekeeper....

中譯和影子跟讀　　　　　🎧 MP3 016

A. In *Getting There*, CBS president and CEO, Leslie Moonves once said "some shows end up being hits, but two out of three fail." and "we get pitched about five hundred television shows a year and only put four new ones on the air." Form these statements, a conclusion can be drawn about fierce competition among different networks and producers. Each season is made up of 10 to 23 episodes with only a tight budget and some shows are truly expensive to make. If a show gets to last to four seasons, it is considered a pretty popular show.

在《勝利並非事事順利》，CBS 總裁兼執行長，萊斯利‧穆維斯曾說過「有些節目最終爆紅，但三個節目之中會有其中兩個失敗」，而「我們每年收到 500 個電視節目的推銷，但僅會有 4 個節目播放」。從這些論述當中，可以得出的結論是，在不同的電視台和製作人之間競爭是激烈的。每一季由 10 到 23 集所組成，當中只有很緊的預算，而有些節目製作起來昂貴異常。如果一個電視節目能持續到第 4 季，那麼這個節目會被視為是相當流行的節目了。

B. Since the ending of one season requires the network to continually be willing to finance or support the show or outside investors are acknowledging the potential and thus want to keep pouring money into the show. Otherwise, the show goes dead. At another instance, fans begging for the show to be back sometimes will work.

既然一季的結束需要電視台持續地願意資助或者支持這個節目或是有其他外部投資客認可這個節目的潛力，而因此想要持續的在節目製作上投入資金。否則，這個節目就會行將就木。在其他時候，劇迷們乞求讓電視劇續播有時候會奏效。

C. Good ratings are the guarantee for the show to last, especially the first few episodes. Some shows are ruthlessly killed and are getting replaced by a back-up, if the first few episodes are not popular. How to attract audiences in the first few episodes is the key, and research in the success of the show has included two successful shows that adopt the same strategy to make the show appealing. The two shows include *Damages* and *Suits*. Both are cliffhangers in the very first episode that consists of the interview scenes. Since everyone has to go to the interview throughout their whole life, audiences want to know how to nail the interview. What makes them glued to the set or Netflix is the riveting scene in which the outcome of the interview cannot be predicted.

Test 2

1
TEST

2
TEST
Reading Passage 1

3
TEST

4
TEST

具有好的收視率是讓電視節目能持續的保證，特別是在前幾集的時候。有些電視節目被殘酷地砍掉並且被備用節目替補了，如果前幾集沒有那麼受歡迎的時候。如何在前幾集就吸引觀眾就是關鍵所在，而節目成功的研究包含了兩個成功的電視節目，兩者採用了相同的策略以讓電視節目吸引人。兩個電視節目包含了《金權遊戲》和《金裝律師》。兩者都是在前幾集就高潮迭起，且包含了面試場景。既然在人的一生中，每個人都必須要參加面試，觀眾會想要知道如何在面試中勝出。能讓他們目不轉睛地看電視或 Netflix 的是引人入勝的情節，無法預測出面試的結果為何。

D. In *Damages*, Ellen Parsons is an outstanding law graduate who goes on an interview at Hollis Nye's law firm, and after the chat, the firm is ready to discuss further details and benefits with Ellen, but is shocked by the fact that Ellen is eyeing another prestigious law firm, Hewes & Associates. But Hewes & Associates, based on its reputation, can have anyone whether it is a seasoned senior lawyer or a newly graduate whose ability is better than Ellen. Yet Ellen goes to the scheduled interview where she meets affable Tom, who is the friend of Patty and a senior partner of the company. Tom is cordial and candid, unlike other interviews who will employ different interview strategies during the interview. He even gives the advice to Ellen to help her better prepared for the ultimate interview with the boss, Patty. Things go well until Tom announces the time of the scheduled interview, which is on Saturday. Ellen is astounded to hear the date because her sister's wedding is on the same date. How to choose between a lucrative job that everyone is dying to get in and attending her sister's wedding is what allures audiences to continue watching till the end of the first episode.

在《金權遊戲》中，亞倫‧帕森斯是位傑出的法律畢業生，正參加荷里斯‧奈爾的律師事務所的面試，在談話後，事務所預備要和亞倫談論進一步的細節和津貼，但是卻對於亞倫在著眼於另一間享譽盛名的休斯律師事務所感到震驚。但是休斯律師事務所，基於其名聲，能夠有任何他們想要的候選人，不論是經驗老道的資深律師或是剛畢業且能力好過亞倫的畢業生。而亞倫如期赴約預定的面試排程，在那裡她遇見了和藹可人的湯姆，其也是派蒂的朋友和公司的資深合夥人。湯姆熱情且坦白，不像是其他的面試官，在面試當中會用到不同的面試策略。他甚至給予亞倫建議以幫助她在面對老闆派蒂的面試時，能有著更好的準備。事情進行得很順利，直到湯姆告知預定的面試時間，也就是星期六。亞倫聽到日期後感到驚訝萬分，時程跟她妹妹的婚禮在同一天。在每個人都迫切想要獲得的有錢的工作和她妹妹的婚禮之間如何做出選擇正是吸引觀眾持續觀看直到第一集結束為止。

E. In *Suits*, the first episode of the show consists of several great blends that will get your adrenaline rush going. It starts with the main character Mike Ross illegitimately taking LSAT for others, and he is almost getting caught. But his agility in changing the outfit saves him in the situation. His desperation for money to pay for his grandmother's health expenses leads to his misdemeanor of illegal transporting the marijuana for his friend, Trevor.

在《金裝律師》，第一集的節目中包含了幾個很棒的組合，讓你的腎上腺素上升。節目始於主要的角色麥克·羅斯非法地替其他人代考 LSAT，而他幾乎要被逮到。但是他的靈敏換裝在節骨眼上救了他。他迫切地需要金錢以支付他奶奶的健康費用，這導致他行為不端，替他的朋友吹佛爾非法進行大麻的運送。

F. At the hotel, his observation for each location and signs saves him from getting arrested by the policemen. "Gloves", "The pool is closed", and "the Harvard law interview event" are the key. When he heads toward the scheduled room, he sees two guys outside the room, who obviously are not the waiter and the guest. He verifies their identities by asking questions on what he sees beforehand. Then both sides soon figure each other out, and that leads to a chase. Then he rushes downstairs and heads to the event. There he gets asked a question by the gatekeeper interviewer. She will ask a question and give a facial expression to the interviewer on whether the person is qualified or not. Mike is confronted with the question of "You are five minutes late. Is there a reason that I should let you in". To which, he replies "I'm just trying to ditch the cop. I don't care if you let me in or not." The action earns him the first nod from the female gatekeeper. And there are other great scenarios that will certainly keep audiences intrigued, such as how to get hired by the law firm without a Harvard degree.

在旅館時，他對每個地點和標誌的觀察讓他免於被警察逮捕。「手套」、「泳池是關閉的」以及「哈佛法律面試會場」都是關鍵所在。當他走向預定的房間時，他看到兩個在房間外頭的男子，兩人顯然不是服務生和客人。他藉由詢問他先前所看到的景象以查證。然後，雙方都立即察覺出異樣，那也導致了追逐。然後，他跑下樓朝著活動現場走去。在那裡，他被入口的面試官詢問了一個問題。她會詢問一個問題，緊接著給予另一名面試官一個表情，告知這個人是否符合資格。麥克面臨的問題是「你遲到了五分鐘。有任何理由讓我應該要讓你進來嗎？」。對此，他回答道「我只是要甩掉警察。我不在乎你是否要讓我進來」。這個行為讓他獲得入口的女面試官的首次點頭。而當中還有其他很棒的情節都確實會讓觀眾感到有興趣，例如，沒有哈佛學歷要怎麼獲得律師事務所錄取。

READING PASSAGE 2

You should spend about 20 minutes on **Questions 14-27**, which are based on Reading Passage 2 below.

English Literature Study:
Captain Smollett's Abdication
Is There Something Behind?

A. Details and storylines of *Treasure Island* are no strangers to devotees of Robert Louis Stevenson, but to those who are still on the journey of preparing for a book report and not yet finish reading to the essential part of the fiction, the abdication of all food supplies and stockade can be quite gripping.

B. Both sides of Captain Smollett and Silver have been experiencing ongoing battles. It remains to be inconclusive to say which party will win the brawl, and the situation does not put Captain Smollett's party at any disadvantage, even though there have been occasional wounds and deaths from his man. Then the intense skirmish has led to a horrific scene as can be seen in chapter 22. "Out of the eight man who had fallen in the action, only three still breathed — that one of the pirates who had been shot at the loophole, Hunter, and Captain Smollett; and of these, the first two were as good as dead." The overall condition has been made worse with Jim leaving the injured party without informing any of them. However, Jim's departure can still be viewed as a good thing to team Captain Smollett, if the author has decided to make this kind of arrangement.

C. In Chapter 28, the cliffhanger ensues, as the discovery of the enemy's camp is revealed. Pork, bread, and the cask of cognac, and other buccaneers are found, but there is no trace of the Captain Smollett members. Then Silver mentions about Doctor Livesey's a flag of truce, an indication that Captain Smollett is relinquishing. Therefore, Silver and remaining buccaneers are getting stores, brandy, block-house, and the firewood. The knowing of the situation emboldens Jim to confess his previous concealment in the apple barrel and other things, although this does not change anything.

D. A great hint has been given in Chapter 30 On Parole. "There is a kind of fate in this." "You found out the plot, you found Ben Gunn – the best deed that ever you did, or will do though you live to ninety." The previous arrangement of Jim's exodus is a great save for all; otherwise, there would not be any ship for them to leave the island. The location of the ship is also revealed by Jim that she lies in North Inlet. The treasure still needs the transportation to ship back to their own country to be valuable. What remains clueless and suspicious to the readers and Silver is the departure of Captain Smollett's remaining members and the offering of the chart of the Treasure Island.

E. The malaria is also a great insinuation to decipher the cause and effect of some of the decisions made by Captain Smollett. On Treasure Island, there is malaria, and the disease can cause fever and tiredness. However, in acute instances, coma and death can occur, and the team Silver does not have a doctor. Even if there is a doctor, in the team Captain Smollett, medical treatment is not as easy as it deems nowadays. Captain Smollett does not have to initiate a physical combat to Silver. Letting the malaria does the trick of its own is even easier.

F. It is announced in Chapter 33 The Fall of a Chieftain that Ben's Gunn's cave is a great insulation to the malaria, so it makes sense to give up the block-house. As for the food supplies, Ben Gunn also has the goats' meat that is brined, a great preservation technique that provides long-enduring food for the team. Therefore, the team Captain Smollett does not need pork and bread on their previous block-house. Ben's Gunn's cave also serves as a great place to store all the gold. The digging of the gold even happens two months before the arrival of the *Hispaniola*. Inside the cave, there is even fresh water, which is quite essential to those treasure-hunters who want to spend long days roaming on the island searching for Flint's treasure.

G. Now all the dots have been connected, and attainment of the Flint's treasure requires Jim, Ben Gunn, luck, and other factors combined. The tale of the *Treasure Island* will always be in the hearts of young children and those who are fans of the pirate story because it is truly a classic.

Questions 14-17

Reading Passage 2 has seven paragraphs, A-G

Which paragraph contains the following information?

Write the correct letter, A-G, in boxes 14-17 on your answer sheet.

NB You may use any letter more than once.

14 mention of a storage that can stash the sweet and fleshy product

15 mention of the time of the excavation of the precious metal

16 mention of an effortless way to triumph

17 mention of the map of the Flint's treasure

Questions 18-21

Complete the summary below

Choose No More Than One Word from the passage for each answer

Write your answers in boxes 18-21 on your answer sheet.

To get Flint's treasure, **18.**_____ is considered necessary on the island. Ben Gunn's cave not only serves as a great place to keep the treasure, but also a great **19.**_____ to the illness. Even with a doctor on the team, malaria can be hard to tackle. The symptoms include **20.**_____ and tiredness. Domesticated ruminant mammals that are **21.**_____ can provide the team Captain Smollett with enough food, so that they no longer need pork, bread, and the cask of cognac.

Questions 22-23

Do the following statements agree with the information given in the Reading Passage 2?

In boxes 22-23 on your answer sheet, write

> **TRUE**- if the statement agrees with the information
> **FALSE**- if the statement contradicts the information
> **NOT GIVEN**- if there is no information on this

22. During the fight, two participants are dying, according to the quote.
23. Doctor Livesey is mad at Jim for leaving the party without telling them.

Questions 24-27

Complete each sentence with the correct ending, A- I below. Write the correct letter, A- I, in boxes 24-27on your answer sheet.

24 Readers and Silver have no knowledge about

25 Readers are unable to make the prediction about

26 Amalgamated efforts can fulfill the dream of getting

27 The situation on the island can be reversed by knowing

A the Flint's treasure

B the exodus of Captain Smollett's captain crews

C the concealment of Jim in the apple barrel

D the location of the ship

E the fight between two parties

F the location of the treasure

G the Doctor Livesey's a flag of truce

H the cure for the malaria

I the disease on the island

Reading Passage 2

05 ｜英國文學＋心理學
《*Treasure Island*》

船長為何願意放棄一切並把豐碩的物資交給西爾佛和他的黨羽呢？

在答題前第一個步驟是先快速掃視題目題型並快速制定答題策略，這篇中有四個題型，加上有完成句子配對題所以較難答，是目前難度較高的一篇試題。

◆ 先快速掃描 14-17 的關鍵字，然後答 14-23 題，最後答完成句子配對題。可以在閱讀到第二段時，找到判斷題**第 22 題**的對應點，During the fight, two participants are dying, according to the quote，對應到"Out of the eight man who had fallen in the action, only three still breathed – that one of the pirates who had been shot at the loophole, Hunter, and Captain Smollett; and of these, the first two were as good as dead."知道其中兩人是瀕死的，故**答案為 True**。

◆ 接著在第三段也就是 C 段落中 The knowing of the situation emboldens Jim to confess his previous concealment in the apple barrel and other things, although this does not change anything.，the apple barrel 對應到第 14 題的 a storage that can stash the sweet and fleshy product，故第**14 題答案為 C**。

◆ 接著在 D 段落中 What remains clueless and suspicious to the readers and Silver is the departure of Captain Smollett's remaining members and the offering of the chart of the Treasure Island. ，可以對應到 the map of the Flint's treasure，chart 就是 map，Flint's treasure 就是金銀島上的寶藏，故第 **17** 題要選 **D**。

◆ 接著看到 E 段落，Captain Smollett does not have to initiate a physical combat to Silver. Letting the malaria does the trick of its own is even easier. ，可以得知根本不用戰鬥就能不戰而勝的方法，這點對應到第 16 題的 an effortless way to triumph，故第 **16** 題要答 **E**。

◆ 接著看到 F 段落，The digging of the gold even happens two months before the arrival of the *Hispaniola*. ，可以得知挖掘的時間點，即 the time of the excavation of the precious metal，故第 **15** 題要選 **F**。

◆ 答這個段落時也能順便答摘要題的部分，To get Flint's treasure, **18.**_____ is considered necessary on the island. ，因為是亂序出題所以要一直看到 The digging of the gold even happens two months before the arrival of the *Hispaniola*. Inside the cave, there is even fresh water, which is quite essential to those treasure-hunters who want to spend long days roaming on the island searching for Flint's treasure.，故答案為 **fresh water**。

◆ 第 **19** 題，Ben's Gunn's cave not only serves as a great place to keep the treasure, but also a great **19._____** to the illness.對應到 it is announced in Chapter 33 The Fall of a Chieftain that Ben's Gunn's cave is a great insulation to the malaria, so it makes sense to give up the block-house.答案很明顯是 **insulation**，其中 illness 對應到 malaria。

◆ 第 **20** 題，Even with a doctor on the team, malaria can be hard to tackle. The symptoms include **20._____** and tiredness.，這題要往回看到 E 段落中的，On Treasure Island, there is malaria, and the disease can cause fever and tiredness.答案很明顯是 **fever**。

◆ 第 **21** 題，Domesticated ruminant mammals that are **21._____** can provide the team Captain Smollett with enough food, so that they no longer need pork, bread, and the cask of cognac.對應到 As for the food supplies, Ben Gunn also has the goats' meat that is brined, a great preservation technique that provides long-enduring food for the team.，當中 goat 換成了 Domesticated ruminant mammals，空格處要填 **brined**。

◆ 最後剩完成句子這四題，**24** Readers and Silver have no knowledge about，要對應到 D 段落尾的，What remains clueless and suspicious to the **readers and Silver** is the departure of Captain Smollett's remaining members and the offering of the chart of the Treasure Island.，故**答案要選 B** the exodus of Captain Smollett's captain crews，他們對船長的船員的出走部分是一無所知的。

◆ 第 **25** 題，**25** Readers are unable to make the prediction about，這點對應到 B 段落開頭處的 It remains to be inconclusive to say which party will win the brawl, and the situation does not put Captain Smollett's party in any disadvantage, even though there have been occasional wounds and deaths from his man.，**故要選 E** the fight between two parties，讀者沒辦法推斷出最後雙方是誰會勝出。

◆ 第 **26** 題，**26** Amalgamated efforts can fulfill the dream of getting，這題有些難，但可以在最後一段 now all the dots have been connected, and attainment of the Flint's treasure requires Jim, Ben Gunn, luck, and other factors combined.找到線索，**故要選 A** the Flint's treasure。是需要這些綜合因素才能成功獲取寶藏並帶回他們居住的國家。

◆ 第 27 題，27 The situation on the island can be reversed by knowing，I the disease on the island。可點可以在 E 段落中找到答案。The malaria is also a great insinuation to decipher the cause and effect of some of the decisions made by Captain Smollett. On Treasure Island, there is malaria, and the disease can cause fever and tiredness. However, in acute instances, coma and death can occur, and the team Silver does not have a doctor. Even if there is a doctor, in the team Captain Smollett, medical treatment is not as easy as it deems nowadays. Captain Smollett does not have to initiate a physical combat to Silver. Letting the malaria does the trick of its own is even easier.，瘧疾是關鍵因素，當中還包含了可以靠疾病不戰而勝的部分，**故要選 I**。

Test 2

MP3 017

TEST 1

TEST 2 Reading Passage 2

TEST 3

TEST 4

聽讀整合 **TEST 2 P2**

Details and **1.**_____ of *Treasure Island* are no strangers to **2.**_____ of Robert Louis Stevenson, but to those who are still on the journey of preparing for a book report and not yet finish reading to the **3.**_____ part of the fiction, the **4.**____ _____ of all food supplies and stockade can be quite gripping.

Both sides of Captain Smollett and Silver have been experiencing ongoing battles. It remains to be inconclusive to say which party will win the **5.**_____, and the situation does not put Captain Smollett's party at any **6.**_____, even though there have been occasional wounds and deaths from his man. Then the intense **7.**_____ has led to a horrific scene as can be seen in chapter 22. "Out of the eight man who had fallen in the action, only three still breathed – that one of the pirates who had been shot at the **8.**_____, Hunter, and Captain Smollett; and of these, the first two were as good as dead." The overall condition has been made worse with Jim leaving the injured party without **9.**_____ any of them. However, Jim's **10.**____ _____ can still be viewed as a good thing to team Captain Smollett, if the author has decided to make this kind of arrangement.

In Chapter 28, the **11.**_____ ensues, as the discovery of the enemy's camp is revealed. Pork, bread, and the cask of **12.**__ _____, and other buccaneers are found, but there is no trace of the Captain Smollett members. Then Silver mentions about Doctor Livesey's a flag of **13.**_____, an indication that

Captain Smollett is relinquishing. Therefore, Silver and remaining buccaneers are getting stores, brandy, block-house, and the **14.**_____. The knowing of the situation **15.**_____ Jim to confess his previous **16.**_____ in the apple **17.**_____ and other things, although this does not change anything.

...The previous arrangement of Jim's exodus is a great save for all; otherwise, there would not be any ship for them to leave the island. The **18.**_____ of the ship is also revealed by Jim that she lies in North **19.**_____. The treasure still needs the **20.**_____ to ship back to their own country to be **21.**_____. What remains clueless and suspicious to the readers and Silver is the departure of Captain Smollett's remaining members and the offering of the chart of the Treasure Island. The **22.**_____ is also a great **23.**_____ to decipher the cause and effect of some of the decisions made by Captain Smollett. On Treasure Island, there is malaria, and the disease can cause fever and **24.**_____. However, in acute instances, **25.**_____ and death can occur, and the team Silver does not have a doctor. Even if there is a doctor, in the team Captain Smollett, medical **26.**_____ is not as easy as it deems nowadays....

It is announced in Chapter 33 The Fall of a Chieftain that Ben's Gunn's **27.**_____ is a great insulation to the malaria, so it makes sense to give up the block-house. As for the food **28.**_____, Ben Gunn also has the goats' meat that is **29.**_____, a great preservation technique that provides **30.**_____ food for the team. Therefore, the team Captain Smollett does not need pork and bread on their previous block-house. Ben's Gunn's cave also serves as a great place to store all the gold. The digging of the gold even happens two months before the arrival of the *Hispaniola*. Inside the cave, there is even fresh water, which is quite essential to those treasure-hunters who want to spend long days **31.**_____ on the island searching for Flint's treasure. Now all the dots have been connected, and **32.**__ _____ of the Flint's treasure requires Jim, Ben Gunn, luck, and other factors combined. The tale of the *Treasure Island* will always be in the hearts of young children and those who are fans of the pirate story because it is truly a classic.

A. Details and storylines of *Treasure Island* are no strangers to devotees of Robert Louis Stevenson, but to those who are still on the journey of preparing for a book report and not yet finish reading to the essential part of the fiction, the abdication of all food supplies and stockade can be quite gripping.

羅伯特‧路易斯‧史蒂文森的愛好者想必對《金銀島》的細節和故事情節並不陌生，但是對於仍在準備書籍報告的途中，且尚未讀完小說重要部份的人來說，放棄所有食物補給和城寨可能是相當扣人心弦的。

B. Both sides of Captain Smollett and Silver have been experiencing ongoing battles. It remains to be inconclusive to say which party will win the brawl, and the situation does not put Captain Smollett's party at any disadvantage, even though there have been occasional wounds and deaths from his man. Then the intense skirmish has led to a horrific scene as can be seen in chapter 22. "Out of the eight man who had fallen in the action, only three still breathed – that one of the pirates who had been shot at the loophole, Hunter, and Captain Smollett; and of these, the first two were as good as dead." The overall condition has been made worse with Jim leaving the injured party without informing any of them. However, Jim's departure can still be viewed as a good thing to team Captain Smollett, if the author has decided to make this kind of arrangement.

史莫列特船長和西爾佛雙方一直經歷著不間斷的戰鬥。哪一方會贏得爭鬥是無法下定論的，而且情勢並未讓史莫列特船長處於任何不利的處境，即使他那方的人員也持續有個零星的傷亡出現。然後，激烈的鬥爭已經導致了在第 22 章中所能目睹的可怕場景了。「在八名受傷的人員中，只有三個人還有呼吸-透過槍孔被射中的海盜、杭特和史莫列特船長，前兩人也幾乎瀕死」。更因為吉姆在未告知他們的情況下離隊讓整體情勢變得更糟了。然而，吉姆的離開對史莫列特船長的團隊來說仍可視為是件好事。

C. In Chapter 28, the cliffhanger ensues, as the discovery of the enemy's camp is revealed. Pork, bread, and the cask of cognac, and other buccaneers are found, but there is no trace of the Captain Smollett members. Then Silver mentions about Doctor Livesey's a flag of truce, an indication that Captain Smollett is relinquishing. Therefore, Silver and remaining buccaneers are getting stores, brandy, block-house, and the firewood. The knowing of the situation emboldens Jim to confess his previous concealment in the apple barrel and other things, although this does not change anything.

在第 28 章，高潮迭起接續著，隨著發現敵營的事情揭露了出來。發現豬肉、麵包、一桶白蘭地和其他海盜，但是卻沒有史莫列特船長成員們的蹤跡。緊接著，西爾佛提到理夫西醫生的休戰旗，暗示著史莫列特船長的棄守。因此，西爾佛和僅存的海盜們獲得了物資、白蘭地、木屋和柴薪。知道這個情況讓吉姆膽大包天的坦誠相告他先前將東西藏在裝蘋果的木桶和其他事情，儘管此舉無法改變任何事情。

D. A great hint has been given in Chapter 30 On Parole. "There is a kind of fate in this." "You found out the plot, you found Ben Gunn – the best deed that ever you did, or will do though you live to ninety." The previous arrangement of Jim's exodus is a great save for all; otherwise, there would not be any ship for them to leave the island. The location of the ship is also revealed by Jim that she lies in North Inlet. The treasure still needs the transportation to ship back to their own country to be valuable. What remains clueless and suspicious to the readers and Silver is the departure of Captain Smollett's remaining members and the offering of the chart of the Treasure Island.

在第 30 章俘虜宣言中能獲得很大的暗示。「命運似乎註定如此」。「你發現了盜匪們的計畫，還找到了班‧剛恩，那是你這輩子做過最厲害的事情了，即便你活到 90 歲時也一樣」。先前吉姆出走的安排對所有人來說卻是大解救，否則就沒有船能讓他們離開金銀島了。吉姆也揭露了船的位置，位於北方內灘上。寶藏仍需要船隻將其運送回他們的國家才能彰顯出其價值連城。對讀者和西爾佛萊說，仍舊毫無頭緒和令人起疑的是史莫列特船長僅存成員的出走和交出金銀島的地圖。

E. The malaria is also a great insinuation to decipher the cause and effect of some of the decisions made by Captain Smollett. On Treasure Island, there is malaria, and the disease can cause fever and tiredness. However, in acute instances, coma and death can occur, and the team Silver does not have a doctor. Even if there is a doctor, in the team Captain Smollett, medical treatment is not as easy as it deems nowadays. Captain Smollett does not have to initiate a physical combat to Silver. Letting the malaria does the trick of its own is even easier.

瘧疾也是一個很大的暗示，以解密史莫列特船長所做的決定這中間的來龍去脈。在金銀島上存在著瘧疾，這個疾病能導致發燒和疲憊。然而，在急性的情況下，會出現昏迷和死亡的徵兆，而且西爾佛的團隊甚至沒有醫生。即使在史莫列特船長的團隊上有醫生，醫療治療並不像現今這樣容易。史莫列特船長甚至不需要對西爾佛發起實體戰鬥。讓瘧疾發揮作用終結西爾佛甚至更簡單。

F. It is announced in Chapter 33 The Fall of a Chieftain that Ben's Gunn's cave is a great insulation to the malaria, so it makes sense to give up the block-house. As for the food supplies, Ben Gunn also has the goats' meat that is brined, a great preservation technique that provides long-enduring food for the team. Therefore, the team Captain Smollett does not need pork and bread on their previous block-house. Ben's Gunn's cave also serves as a great place to store all the gold. The digging of the gold even happens two months before the arrival of the *Hispaniola*. Inside the cave, there is even fresh water, which is quite essential to those treasure-hunters who want to spend long days roaming on the island searching for Flint's treasure.

在第 33 章首領殞落中透露，班‧剛恩的洞穴是阻絕瘧疾的好處所，所以放棄城寨是很合理的。關於食物補給，班‧剛恩也有鹽制的山羊肉，一個極佳的保存方式，提供了團隊耐久的食物。因此，史莫列特船長並不需要他們先前城寨中的豬肉和麵包。班‧剛恩的洞穴也提供了保存黃金的好地點。挖掘黃金這件事情甚至發生於 *Hispaniola* 號抵達的兩個月前。

在洞穴裡頭，甚至有新鮮的水，這對那些尋寶的賞金獵人意欲在島上長時間待著尋找弗林特的寶藏來說是至關重要的。

G. Now all the dots have been connected, and attainment of the Flint's treasure requires Jim, Ben Gunn, luck, and other factors combined. The tale of the *Treasure Island* will always be in the hearts of young children and those who are fans of the pirate story because it is truly a classic.

現在所有的線索都串成一塊了，獲得弗林特的寶藏需要吉姆、班·剛恩、運氣和其他因素的結合才能成事。《金銀島》這個故事將永遠會存在年幼的小孩以及那些海盜故事迷心中，因為它確實是個經典之作。

You should spend about 20 minutes on **Questions 28-40**, which are based on Reading Passage 3 below.

The Vicissitudes of Life: How to See Things in a Different Light

A. In life, we will encounter frustrations and despair from time to time, and life just doesn't go our way. As a saying goes, "life does not always give us the joys we want." Some are beyond our control, such as loss of a loved one, an accident, and so on. Others are small choices added up, eventually being something that we cannot control. Research in dealing with adversity and frustrations has taken us to see things in a different way so that we can still see the silver lining in things.

B. In *Getting There*, Anderson Cooper mentions "anytime you experience traumatic loss early on it changes who you are and drastically affects your view of the world." The statement has a powerful message for those who have endured a great loss of the loved one. God has given us the life lesson to endure the worst thing that ensues. If we can see bad things in a positive way, there is nothing that we cannot cope with later in life.

C. In *Way of the Peaceful Warrior*, a promising young athlete, named Danny, is encountered with a car accident that puts him in an emergence room. It is a life lesson that everyone has not clearly been prepared for. Joy shares the story from Socrates to Danny. There is wisdom in the story of an old man and his son. "Who knows whether it is bad luck or good luck." That is really hard to distinguish. Connotations are certainly abundant in that sentence. Lots of small things that happen in the single story that you cannot tell which thing happening is good or bad for you at the moment. Ultimately, Joy says "everything has a purpose, Danny; it's for you to make the use of it."

D. This can also be served as a good way to interpret what happened to Anderson's father and his brother. His father didn't make it during the heart surgery and his brother chose to commit suicide. We can hardly make a distinction to say it is a bad thing for us, even though we will certainly encounter grief. Joy doesn't want Danny to interpret the car accident as an accident. What we can do is make the most of it, just like what Joy says. (A great perennial classic, *Gone with the Wind* was produced during the author, Margaret Mitchell's recovery from an automobile accident.) We don't have to see things in a bad way. A various interpretation can exhibit a great difference in things.

E. In *Ugly Betty*, Wilhelmina Slater also comes across an adversity later in life. Slater used to work for a fashion icon, Fey Sommer, by using her name Wanda, and she doesn't want others to know about it. It was her distant past. She has worked her way up the corporate ladder by using multiple stratagems and eventually gets to be the editor-in-chief of Mode magazine. She and Daniel have the equal authority and each with a 50% of the share of the company. Numerous things happen later in her life, and that makes her question about life. First, the CFO Connor steals money from the company by making several transfers. She has been beguiling by Connor's charm, and pays no attention to what the assistant has to say. The budget doesn't add up right.

F. Even though later Harley pours into enough money for the company to operate, her influence for the company has begun to wane. She surreptitiously notices a great opportunity from another magazine, thinking that she will get the job after her last photoshoot at the Bahamas. Unfortunately, her opponent surprisingly gets the job. She learns the news from watching TV in the room, and her emotions are aggravated by what her enemy says "How can a girl get so lucky". She is obviously all alone, whereas her opponent has a loving husband who supports her, and a beautiful daughter who stands by her side when she announces the news of taking the offer from the job. It is a series of her choices from the past. She puts all her attention to work, neglecting her daughters for a long time. Later, she is found on the beach, gluttonously eating the hamburger, and she doesn't care if she will be spotted by the paparazzi, a sharp contrast to what she used to do to the assistant. She clearly hits the rock bottom. Will things turn around?

Questions 28-31

Reading Passage 3 has SIX paragraphs, A-F

Which paragraph contains the following information?

Write the correct letter, A-F, in boxes 28-31 on your answer sheet.

NB You may use any letter more than once.

28 mention of the line that is blurring to discriminate

29 mention of ungovernable factors make life morose

30 mention of one's allurement that bamboozles someone

31 mention of a course of action that is damaging

Questions 32-40

Look at the following statements (Questions 32-40) and the list of books below.

Match each statement with the correct book, A-H

Write the correct letter, A-H, in boxes 32-40 on your answer sheet.

NB You may use any letter more than once.

32 there is an intention for all things

33 devours junk food at the cost of a public image

34 was once a legendary figure

35 a trauma will dramatically change one's perception

36 one's last strength leaves someone

37 remarkable achievements accomplished during the hospitalization

38 embezzles cash through the bank

39 clandestinely checks another opportunity

40 successfully getting both A and B

List of people

A Wilhelmina Slater

B Anderson Cooper

C Joy

D Margaret Mitchell

E Anderson's father

F Connor

G Fey Sommer

H opponent of Wilhelmina Slater

解析

06 ｜哲學＋人生觀

《*Ugly Betty*》、《*Getting There*》和《*Way of the Peaceful Warrior*》

人生的酸甜苦辣和如何面對逆境和挫折

　　在答題前第一個步驟是先快速掃視題目題型並快速制定答題策略，在這篇很快可以看到配對題和段落細節題，不過段落細節題有時候蠻隱晦不太好答，可以快速掃描並記憶相關關鍵字，邊閱讀邊答。

◆ **第 35 題**，Anderson Cooper mentions "anytime you experience traumatic loss early on it changes who you are and drastically affects your view of the world." 對應到 a trauma will dramatically change one's perception，故答案要選 **B**。

◆ **第 32 題**，接著讀到 C 段落，可以在 C 段落找到 Ultimately, Joy says "everything has a purpose, Danny; it's for you to make the use of it." 對應到 there is an intention for all things，故答案要選 **C**。

◆ 緊接著讀到 D 段落，作者以比較隱晦的方式表達死亡 one's last strength leaves someone，引申出 Anderson's father 的手術

失敗過世，故第 **36** 題要選 **E**。

◆ 該段落中還有一個考點，尤其是在括號內的都是常考點，別忽略掉或跳過了。(A great perennial classic, *Gone with the Wind* was produced during the author, Margaret Mitchell's recovery from an automobile accident.)，這點可以對應到 remarkable achievements accomplished during the hospitalization，故第 **37** 題要選 **D**。

◆ 接著在 E 段落中找到，Slater used to work for a fashion icon, Fey Sommer, by using her name Wanda, and she doesn't want others to know about it. It was her distant past.對應到 was once a legendary figure，故第 34 題**答案要選 G**。

◆ 接著讀到 CFO 的部分，First, the CFO Connor steals money from the company by making several transfers，這部分對應到 embezzles cash through the bank，make several transfers 的地方在銀行，embezzle 對應到 steal money，故第 38 題**答案要選 F**。

◆ 接著在 F 段落，She surreptitiously notices a great opportunity from another magazine, thinking that she will get the job after her last photoshoot at the Bahamas.這部分

對應到 **39** clandestinely checks another opportunity，故第 39 題答案要選 **A**。**clandestinely** 等同於 **surreptitiously**。

- **第 40 題**較為隱晦，Unfortunately, her opponent surprisingly gets the job. She learns the news from watching TV in the room, and her emotions are aggravated by what her enemy says "How can a girl get so lucky". She is obviously all alone, whereas her opponent has a loving husband who supports her, and a beautiful daughter who stands by her side when she announces the news of taking the offer from the job. ，但仍可以推斷出她的對手是兩者兼得的，家庭和事業都成功的出色女性，對應到 **40** successfully getting both A and B，故第 **40** 題要選 **H**。

- 在這段還有一個訊息點，在 Later, she is found on the beach, gluttonously eating the hamburger, and she doesn't care if she will be spotted by the paparazzi, a sharp contrast to what she used to do to the assistant. ，這點對應到第 33 題的 devours junk food at the cost of a public image，其中 burger 對應到 junk food，devours 對應到 gluttonous，故**答案為 A**。

- 最後來答較隱晦的這四題，**28** mention of the line that is blurring to discriminate，這部分可以對應到 C 段落中的"Who knows whether it is bad luck or good luck." We can hardly make a distinction to say it is a bad thing for us, even though we will certainly encounter grief. ，是很難去區分的，當中 **discriminate** 等於 **distinction**，故答案為 **C**。

◆ **第 29 題，29** mention of ungovernable factors make life morose 則是在 A 段落中可以找到 As a saying goes, "life does not always give us the joys we want." Some are beyond our control, such as loss of a loved one, an accident, and so on. ，這些都是無法控制的因素，故**答案要選 A**。

◆ **第 30 題，30** mention of one's allurement that bamboozles someone，bamboozle 指的是迷惑或哄騙，這點可以在 E 段落中找到，First, the CFO Connor steals money from the company by making several transfers. She is beguiled by Connor's charm, and pays no attention to what the assistant has to say. The budget doesn't add up right. ，當中 **charm** 等同於 **allurement**，故**答案要選 E**。

◆ **第 31 題，31** mention of a course of action that is damaging，對應到 D 段落中的 His father didn't make it during the heart surgery and his brother chose to commit suicide. ，當中 a course of action 就是行為 damaging 指自殺的傷害，其實敘述就是隱晦的表達出 commit suicide，故**答案要選 D**。

聽讀整合 TEST 2 P3

In life, we will encounter **1.**_____ and despair from time to time, and life just doesn't go our way....Others are small **2.**_____ _____ added up, eventually being something that we cannot control. Research in dealing with **3.**_____ and frustrations has taken us to see things in a different way so that we can still see the silver lining in things.

In *Getting There*, Anderson Cooper mentions "anytime you experience **4.**_____ loss early on it changes who you are and drastically affects your view of the world." The statement has a powerful **5.**_____ for those who have endured a great loss of the loved one. God has given us the life lesson to endure the worst thing that ensues....In *Way of the Peaceful Warrior*, a **6.**_____ young athlete, named Danny, is encountered with a car accident that puts him in an **7.**_____ room. It is a life lesson that everyone has not clearly been prepared for. Joy shares the story from Socrates to Danny. There is **8.**_____ in the story of an old man and his son. "Who knows whether it is bad luck or good luck." That is really hard to distinguish. **9.**_____ _____ are certainly abundant in that sentence. Lots of small things that happen in the single story that you cannot tell which thing happening is good or bad for you at the moment. Ultimately, Joy says "everything has a **10.**_____, Danny; it's for you to make the use of it."

This can also be served as a good way to **11.**_____ what happened to Anderson's father and his brother. His father didn't make it during the heart **12.**_____ and his brother chose to commit **13.**_____. We can hardly make a **14.**_____ __ to say it is a bad thing for us, even though we will certainly encounter **15.**_____....What we can do is make the most of it, just like what Joy says. (A great perennial classic, *Gone with the Wind* was **16.**_____ during the author, Margaret Mitchell's **17.**_____ from an automobile accident.) We don't have to see things in a bad way. A various **18.**_____ can exhibit a great difference in things.

In *Ugly Betty*, Wilhelmina Slater also comes across an adversity later in life. Slater used to work for a **19.**_____ icon, Fey Sommer, by using her name Wanda, and she doesn't want others to know about it. It was her **20.**_____ past. She has worked her way up the **21.**_____ ladder by using multiple **22.**_____ and eventually gets to be the editor-in-chief of Mode magazine. She and Daniel have the equal **23.**_____ and each with a 50% of the share of the company. **24.**_____ __ things happen later in her life, and that makes her question about life. First, the CFO Connor **25.**_____ money from the company by making several **26.**_____. She has been **27.**__ _____ by Connor's charm, and pays no attention to what the assistant has to say. The **28.**_____ doesn't add up right.

Even though later Harley pours into enough money for the company to operate, her influence for the company has begun to wane. She **29.**_____ notices a great opportunity from another magazine, thinking that she will get the job after her last photoshoot at the Bahamas. Unfortunately, her opponent surprisingly gets the job. She learns the news from watching TV in the room, and her **30.**_____ are aggravated by what her enemy says "How can a girl get so lucky". She is obviously all alone, whereas her opponent has a loving husband who supports her, and a beautiful daughter who stands by her side when she announces the news of taking the offer from the job. It is a series of her choices from the past. She puts all her attention to work, **31.**_____ her daughters for a long time. Later, she is found on the beach, **32.**_____ eating the hamburger, and she doesn't care if she will be spotted by the paparazzi, a sharp contrast to what she used to do to the assistant. She clearly hits the rock bottom. Will things turn around?

A. In life, we will encounter frustrations and despair from time to time, and life just doesn't go our way. As a saying goes, "life does not always give us the joys we want." Some are beyond our control, such as loss of a loved one, an accident, and so on. Others are small choices added up, eventually being something that we cannot control. Research in dealing with adversity and frustrations has taken us to see things in a different way so that we can still see the silver lining in things.

在生活中，我們偶爾會碰到挫折和絕望，而生活不會照我們要的方式走。俗話說：「生活並不總是給予我們所想要的喜悅」。有些事情超過了我們的控制範疇，例如失去摯愛、意外等等的。另一些卻是些微的選擇逐漸積累而成的，最終演變成一些我們無法控制的事情。處理逆境和挫折的研究已經帶領我們以不同的方式去看待事情，如此一來，我們就能夠看到困境中的一絲希望。

B. In *Getting There*, Anderson Cooper mentions "anytime you experience traumatic loss early on it changes who you are and drastically affects your view of the world." The statement has a powerful message for those who have endured a great loss of the loved one. God has given us the life lesson to endure the worst thing that ensues. If we can see bad things in a positive way, there is nothing that we cannot cope with later in life.

在《勝利並非事事順利》，安德森·庫柏提及「你在人生初期的任何時候，遭逢失去的創傷，此會改變你並且急劇地改變了你的世界觀」。此陳述對那些已遭逢失去摯愛的人來說是個強而有力的訊息。上帝已給予我們人生的課題以讓我們能接著面對接下來更糟的狀況。如果我們能夠以正向的方式去看待壞事，在人生後面的階段，沒有什麼事情會是我們無法處理的。

C. In *Way of the Peaceful Warrior*, a promising young athlete, named Danny, is encountered with a car accident that puts him in an emergence room. It is a life lesson that everyone has not clearly been prepared for. Joy shares the story from Socrates to Danny. There is wisdom in the story of an old man and his son. "Who knows whether it is bad luck or good luck." That is really hard to distinguish. Connotations are certainly abundant in that sentence. Lots of small things that happen in the single story that you cannot tell which thing happening is good or bad for you at the moment. Ultimately, Joy says "everything has a purpose, Danny; it's for you to make the use of it."

在《深夜加油站遇見蘇格拉底》，一位前程似錦的年輕運動員，名叫丹尼，遭遇了一場汽車意外，這讓他進了急診室。這是每個人顯然都並未準備好要面對的人生課題。喬伊將蘇格拉底的故事分享給丹尼。一位老年男子和他兒子的故事有著智慧混在其中。「誰知道這是壞運還是好運」。那真的很難做出區隔。那句話中顯然富有寓意在其中。在單一故事中所發生的許多小事情，你都無法去分辨出所發生的事情對你當下來說會是好事或壞事。最終，喬伊說道「丹尼，每件事情的發生都是有目的的，全看你要如何運用它」。

D. This can also be served as a good way to interpret what happened to Anderson's father and his brother. His father didn't make it during the heart surgery and his brother chose to commit suicide. We can hardly make a distinction to say it is a bad thing for us, even though we will certainly encounter grief. Joy doesn't want Danny to interpret the car accident as an accident. What we can do is make the most of it, just like what Joy says. (A great perennial classic, *Gone with the Wind* was produced during the author, Margaret Mitchell's recovery from an automobile accident.) We don't have to see things in a bad way. A various interpretation can exhibit a great difference in things.

這也能成為詮釋發生在安德森父親和哥哥身上的事情的一個好的方法。他父親在心臟手術中過世了，還有他哥哥選擇自殺。我們幾乎很難去區分這件事情對我們來說是件壞事，即使我們確實遭受悲傷的苦楚。喬伊並不想要丹尼將汽車意外視為是一場意外。就像喬伊對丹尼所說的，我們所能做的事情就是充分運用這件事情（《亂世佳人》，一部歷久不衰的經典之作也是創作於作者瑪格麗特‧米歇爾歷經的一場汽車意外的康復中）。我們不需要把事情看成是壞事。對事情不同的詮釋會顯示出截然不同的看法。

E. In *Ugly Betty*, Wilhelmina Slater also comes across an adversity later in life. Slater used to work for a fashion icon, Fey Sommer, by using her name Wanda, and she doesn't want others to know about it. It was her distant past. She has worked her way up the corporate ladder by using multiple stratagems and eventually gets to be the editor-in-chief of Mode magazine. She and Daniel have the equal authority and each with a 50% of the share of the company. Numerous things happen later in her life, and that makes her question about life. First, the CFO Connor steals money from the company by making several transfers. She has been beguiling by Connor's charm, and pays no attention to what the assistant has to say. The budget doesn't add up right.

在《醜女貝蒂》，薇勒米娜·史內特也在人生的後期遭逢了逆境。史內特過去曾在時尚偶像菲·桑默手下辦事，並使用了汪達當作她的名字，但是她卻不想要其他人知道這件事情。這是她的過往。她藉由許多的計謀最終爬升至 Mode 雜誌的主編。她和丹尼爾有著相同的權力，彼此都擁有各 50% 的公司股份。在她生活後期，許多事情發生了，而這使得她開始對生活產生了質疑。首先是，公司的財務長康納藉由幾次的轉帳竊取公司的錢。她被康納的魅力所蒙蔽了，且沒有意識到助理所說的話。預算加總起來不太對。

F. Even though later Harley pours into enough money for the company to operate, her influence for the company has begun to wane. She surreptitiously notices a great opportunity from another magazine, thinking that she will get the job after her last photoshoot at the Bahamas. Unfortunately, her opponent surprisingly gets the job. She learns the news from watching TV in the room, and her emotions are aggravated by what her enemy says "How can a girl get so lucky". She is obviously all alone, whereas her opponent has a loving husband who supports her, and a beautiful daughter who stands by her side when she announces the news of taking the offer from the job. It is a series of her choices from the past. She puts all her attention to work, neglecting her daughters for a long time. Later, she is found on the beach, gluttonously eating the hamburger, and she doesn't care if she will be spotted by the paparazzi, a sharp contrast to what she used to do to the assistant. She clearly hits the rock bottom. Will things turn around?

在更之後，即使哈里注入了足夠的資金讓公司能夠運作，她對公司的影響力開始式微。她暗中注意著另一間雜誌公司的絕佳機會，認為她會在巴哈馬最後一次的相片拍攝後拿到該份工作。不幸的是，她的對手意外地獲得了這份工作。她藉由在房間的電視中觀看到此消息，她的情緒也因為她的對手所說的「怎麼有女人能如此幸運」而加劇。她顯然是孤獨一人，而她的對手有著關愛她的丈夫支持著她，以及有位美麗的女兒，在她得知獲取這份工作的消息時站在她身旁陪伴她。這卻反映出是史奈特過去一系列的選擇。她過去將重心都放在工作上頭，有很長一段時間都忽略了她女兒。後來，史奈特在海灘上被發現，狼吞虎嚥地吃起漢堡，而她不在乎自己是否被狗仔隊拍到此景，與她先前對編輯所做的形成了很大的反差。她顯然到了人生的谷底。但事情會有轉機嗎？

參考答案

Test 2

Reading passage 1 (1-13)

1. B
2. D
3. D
4. C
5. experience
6. affability
7. conflicting
8. lucrative
9. illegitimacy
10. illegally
11. identities
12. closure
13. nod

Reading passage 2 (14-27)

14. C
15. F
16. E
17. D
18. freshwater
19. insulation
20. fever
21. brined
22. True
23. False
24. B
25. E
26. A
27. I

Reading passage 3 (28-40)

28. C
29. A
30. E
31. D
32. C
33. A
34. G
35. B
36. E
37. D
38. F
39. A
40. H

聽讀整合 參考答案

Test 2 P1

1. president
2. pitched
3. television
4. competition
5. producers
6. episodes
7. expensive
8. support
9. acknowledging
10. pouring
11. guarantee
12. ruthlessly
13. audiences
14. adopt
15. appealing
16. cliffhangers
17. nail
18. outcome
19. benefits
20. prestigious
21. reputation
22. seasoned
23. scheduled
24. affable
25. cordial
26. employ
27. ultimate
28. Saturday
29. illegitimately
30. misdemeanor
31. identities
32. downstairs

Test 2 P2

1. storylines
2. devotees
3. essential
4. abdication
5. brawl
6. disadvantage
7. skirmish
8. loophole
9. informing
10. departure
11. cliffhanger
12. cognac
13. truce
14. firewood
15. emboldens
16. concealment
17. barrel
18. location
19. Inlet
20. transportation
21. valuable
22. malaria
23. insinuation
24. tiredness
25. coma
26. treatment
27. cave
28. supplies
29. brined
30. long-enduring
31. roaming
32. attainment

Test 2 P3

1. frustrations
2. choices
3. adversity
4. traumatic
5. message
6. promising
7. emergence
8. wisdom
9. Connotations
10. purpose
11. interpret
12. surgery
13. suicide
14. distinction
15. grief
16. produced
17. recovery
18. interpretation
19. fashion
20. distant
21. corporate
22. stratagems
23. authority
24. Numerous
25. steals
26. transfers
27. beguiling
28. budget
29. surreptitiously
30. emotions
31. neglecting
32. gluttonously

Test 3

篇章概述

07

「三個臭皮匠勝過一個諸葛亮」在此真的不適用，傳說中的A到底是誰呢？

在這篇很快可以看到段落細節題、判斷題和圖表題。先順讀，邊答判斷題和圖表題，也可以一邊找段落細節題。

08

經典文學和暢銷書教你愛得更聰明

在這篇很快可以看到有配對題判斷題和摘要題，可以同步答這三類的題型。

09

八方旅人的遊戲攻略和破關要點

在這篇很快可以看到配對題的部分，配對題大多是依順序出題，所以採取「**順答**」，照文章段落順序閱讀文章並答題。

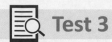

READING PASSAGE 1

You should spend about 20 minutes on **Questions 1-13**, which are based on Reading Passage 1 below.

Pretty Little Liars:
Overturn the Saying
Three Heads Are Better Than One

A. The Halloween scenes of both season 2 and season 3 of *Pretty Little Liars* have been the memorable parts throughout 7 seasons of the show. It is also a good way to understand Allison's character, since her body has been found by the police during the first episode of season 1, leaving most characters and audiences a big puzzle, who is A. The old saying of "Three heads are better than one" is clearly not applied to *Pretty Little Liars*. As the story progresses, A obviously outwits the remaining four girls combined and their friends and family members. Four main roles include Aria, Emily, Hanna, and Spencer.

B. In season 2, before the disappearance of Allison, there was a Halloween party that was hosted by Noel. All liars were anxious to find Allison, and they received a message from Allison, saying that she was in trouble. They eventually left the party and went to the empty macabre house. A search for Allison has begun, and they all held their breath while walking in a terrifying house. Eventually, they entered into a large room where there was no trace of Allison.

C. Then the door unexpectedly closed and was locked. Thereafter, there came the voice of Allison. Allison was seen obviously struggling and fighting with someone outside the room. All girls could only see what was actually going on through the keyhole of the door knob. They swiftly thought of a way of using the smartphone to call 911.

D. However, there were no signals, so there was no way that they could get the help from the police. The scene made audiences' adrenalin rush heightened as Allison kept screaming. So did all liars. The guy was masked, so you cannot figure out the identity. The tension was dramatized as the time went by. Nevertheless, they soon figured that the open window was the way to get out of the house and see what actually happened here. After reentering the house, they found Allison who remained poised and unharmed on an armchair in the room, claiming that it was a mischief. As for the blood, her elucidation was that it was the ketchup. The identity of the costumed person was actually Noel.

E. All girls have been beguiled by Allison, and this is actually the type of the person that Allison is. When they all go back to the real party, Allison makes a gesture to Noel to thank him for portraying the role so that she gets to play the Halloween prank for the girls. Noel nervously explains to Allison that he does not go to the scary house because other things actually came up. The question remains, if Noel does not go to the house, then who, and this terrifies Allison as she begins to search for clues from the party. Apparently, there are multiple people wearing the mask. The real culprit can or cannot be here, and if this person is gunning for Allison or wants to hurt Allison, she does not have the chance to escape.

F. Still Allison has plenty of actions that are questionable, and you might even wonder why she has to do things that way. Apparently, she needs help. There is also a scene where she is with her mother outside the coffee shop. They are congenial, enjoying the dessert and beverage. Then when Allison does not get what she wants, she stops breathing. Her mother disagrees with her having a party at the lake house. It is not until her mother screams "breathe" and agrees with her that she starts breathing. It is like she has been the problematic girl. No parents can handle her.

G. There are numerous questionable behaviors you will find throughout the series, including getting Jenna blind. There is a fire that unexpectedly starts by the girls during season 1.

H. As for the real A, there are several clues in season 1 and season 3. If you have a keen eye for human relationships, you can easily identify those messages. Otherwise, you will be like multiple hornets following the hormone traces, but still cannot find the larder. That is also the writing strategies and narrations that want you to keep meandering and be loyal audiences that glue to the set.

英文試題

Questions 1-7

Questions 1-7

Reading Passage 1 has EIGHT paragraphs, A-H

Which paragraph contains the following information?

Write the correct letter, A-H, in boxes 1-7 on your answer sheet.

NB You may use any letter more than once.

1 mention of a condiment that is served as a prop

2 mention of a regulatory substance produced in an organism

3 mention of agreeableness between two parties

4 mention of the process of taking air into the organ

5 mention of the deprivation of one's perception

6 mention of a gadget that can be useful in danger

7 mention of a gruesome lodge

Questions 8-9

Do the following statements agree with the information given in the Reading Passage 1

In boxes 8-9 on your answer sheet, write

> **TRUE**- if the statement agrees with the information
> **FALSE**- if the statement contradicts the information
> **NOT GIVEN**- if there is no information on this

8. The identity of the costumed person was actually Noel.
9. Allison expresses her gratitude to Noel for portraying the masked person.

Questions 10-13

Label the diagram below

Choose NO MORE THAN TWO WORDS from the passage for each answer.

Write your answers in boxes 10-13 on your answer sheet.

A Halloween Incident

The party was organized by Noel.

They went to the macabre house,
but couldn't find Allison.

The door was locked.

All liars could only witness the phenomenon
through *10.* _____.

The notion of using *11.* _____ was shattered
because there were no signals.

The real identity of the guy remained unknown
because he was *12.* _____.

They figured out the solution of getting out the house.

The reentering scene of the house revealed that Allison
was unharmed and *13.* _____.

解析

07 ｜犯罪＋心理學
《美少女的謊言》

「三個臭皮匠勝過一個諸葛亮」在此真的不適用，傳說中的 A 到底是誰呢？

　　在答題前第一個步驟是先快速掃視題目題型並快速制定答題策略，在這篇很快可以看到段落細節題、判斷題和圖表題。先順讀，邊答判斷題和圖表題，也可以一邊找段落細節題。

◆ 可以先看判斷題**第 8 題**，以 **Noel** 為關鍵字定位回去找答案，對應到 As for the blood, her elucidation was that it was the ketchup. The identity of the costumed person was actually Noel.但是後面其他段落還有關於 Noel 的敘述，When they all go back to the real party, Allison makes a gesture to Noel to thank him for portraying the role so that she gets to play the Halloween prank for the girls. Noel nervously explains to Allison that he does not go the scary house because other things actually came up.，所以 Allison 回應閨密時她認為是 Noel，但後來 Noel 表明自已因為事情耽誤沒有扮演該角色，所以答案要選 **False**。（如果沒有後面這段的敘述的話就要選 **True**。）

◆ 答這題也能順便答**第 1 題**，As for the blood, her elucidation

was that it was the ketchup.的部分可以對應到 a condiment that is served as a prop，女孩們看到的血跡，是 Allison 用番茄醬代替的道具，來充當血跡，**condiment** 指的是**佐料**也就是番茄醬隱晦的改寫，答案為 D。

♦ 這段敘述還能一併答**第 9 題**，When they all go back to the real party, Allison makes a gesture to Noel to thank him for portraying the role so that she gets to play the Halloween prank for the girls. Noel nervously explains to Allison that he does not go the scary house because other things actually came up.，Allison 確實有表達感謝，故**要選 True**。

♦ 接著看到圖表題**第 10 題**的部分，All liars could only witness the phenomenon through 10._____，跟著流程圖的描述看到 C 段落的 All girls could only see what was actually going on through the keyhole of the door knob.，**答案要選 keyhole**。

♦ **第 11 題**，The notion of using 11._____ was shattered because there were no signals.，這部分對應到 They swiftly thought of a way of using the smartphone to call 911.和 however, there were no signals, so there was no way that they could get the help from the police.，這題有改寫過但答案還是蠻容易看出的，**要選 smartphone**。

◆ 第 **12** 題，The real identity of the guy remained unknown because he was **12.** _____ **.** ，這部分對應到 The guy was masked, so you cannot figure out the identity.所以**答案要選 masked**。其中 **remained unknown** 等同於 **cannot figure out the identity**。

◆ 第 **13** 題，The reentering scene of the house revealed that Allison was unharmed and **13.** _____ **.** ，After reentering the house, they found Allison who remained poised and unharmed on an armchair in the room, claiming that it was a mischief. As for the blood, her elucidation was that it was the ketchup. ，**答案很明顯是 poised**。

◆ 接下來要答剩下的六題，**2** mention of a regulatory substance produced in an organism，這題比較隱晦，但還是可以定位到 D 段落中 The scene made audiences' adrenalin rush heightened as Allison kept screaming. ，adrenalin 就是 regulatory substance，故**答案要選 D**。

◆ 第 **3** 題，**3** mention of agreeableness between two parties，接續讀到剛才沒讀到的 F 段落，There is also a scene where she is with her mother outside the coffee shop. They are congenial, enjoying the dessert and beverage. ，congenial 就是關鍵字，且可以對應到 **agreeableness**，故**答案要選 F**。

♦ **第 4 題**，**4** mention of the process of taking air into the organ，也是定位到 F 段落，這篇跟有些試題一樣，有些段落訊息會出現兩次，所以要特別小心。Then when Allison does not get what she wants, she stops breathing. Her mother disagrees with her having a party at the lake house.，可以對應到 breathing，故**答案為 F**。

♦ **第 5 題**，**5** mention of the deprivation of one's perception，接續看到 G 段落，there are numerous questionable behaviors you will find throughout the series, including getting Jenna blind，blind 對應到了 deprivation of one's perception，故第 5 題**答案為 G**。

♦ **第 6 題**，**6** mention of a gadget that can be useful in danger，這點要往回找，在 C 段落的地方可以找到，所以是 They swiftly thought of a way of using the smartphone to call 911.，gadget 指的是 smartphone，故**答案為 C**。

♦ **第 7 題**，也是要往回找，但比較簡單，**7** mention of a gruesome lodge，對應到 They eventually left the party and went to the empty macabre house.，其中 **gruesome** 等同於 **macabre**，故**答案為 B**。

Test 3

MP3 019

TEST 1
TEST 2
TEST 3 Reading Passage 1
TEST 4

聽讀整合 TEST 3 P1

The **1.**_____ scenes of both season 2 and season 3 of *Pretty Little Liars* have been the memorable parts throughout 7 seasons of the show. It is also a good way to understand Allison's character, since her body has been found by the police during the first episode of season 1, leaving most characters and audiences a big **2.**_____, who is A....As the story progresses, A obviously **3.**_____ the remaining four girls combined and their friends and family **4.**_____. Four main roles include Aria, Emily, Hanna, and Spencer.

In season 2, before the **5.**_____ of Allison, there was a Halloween party that was hosted by Noel. All liars were **6.**_____ to find Allison, and they received a **7.**_____ from Allison, saying that she was in trouble. They eventually left the party and went to the empty **8.**_____ house. A search for Allison has begun, and they all held their breath while walking in a **9.**_____ house. Eventually, they entered into a large room where there was no **10.**_____ of Allison.

Then the door unexpectedly closed and was locked. Thereafter, there came the **11.**_____ of Allison. Allison was seen **12.**_____ struggling and fighting with someone outside the room. All girls could only see what was actually going on through the **13.**_____ of the door knob. They **14.**_____ thought of a way of using the **15.**_____ to call 911.

However, there were no **16.**_____, so there was no way that they could get the help from the police. The scene made audiences' **17.**_____ rush **18.**_____ as Allison kept screaming. So did all liars. The guy was masked, so you cannot figure out the **19.**_____. The tension was **20.**_____ as the time went by. Nevertheless, they soon figured that the open **21.**_____ was the way to get out of the house and see what actually happened here. After reentering the house, they found Allison who remained **22.**_____ and unharmed on an **23.**_____ in the room, claiming that it was a **24.**_____ _____. As for the blood, her **25.**_____ was that it was the **26.**_____. The identity of the costumed person was actually Noel.

All girls have been beguiled by Allison, and this is actually the type of the person that Allison is. When they all go back to the real party, Allison makes a gesture to Noel to thank him for **27.**_____ _____ the role so that she gets to play the Halloween prank for the girls....The question remains, if Noel does not go to the house, then who, and this terrifies Allison as she begins to search for **28.**_____ from the party. Apparently, there are multiple people wearing the mask. The real culprit can or cannot be here, and if this person is gunning for Allison or wants to hurt Allison, she does not have the chance to escape.

...Apparently, she needs help. There is also a scene where she is with her mother outside the **29.**_____ shop. They are **30.**_____, enjoying the dessert and beverage. Then when Allison does not get what she wants, she stops breathing. Her mother disagrees with her having a party at the lake house. It is not until her mother screams "breathe" and agrees with her that she starts breathing. It is like she has been the problematic girl. No parents can handle her. There are numerous questionable behaviors you will find throughout the series, including getting Jenna **31.**_____. There is a fire that unexpectedly starts by the girls during season 1.

...If you have a keen eye for human relationships, you can easily identify those messages. Otherwise, you will be like multiple hornets following the **32.**_____ traces, but still cannot find the larder. That is also the writing strategies and narrations that want you to keep meandering and be loyal audiences that glue to the set.

A. The Halloween scenes of both season 2 and season 3 of *Pretty Little Liars* have been the memorable parts throughout 7 seasons of the show. It is also a good way to understand Allison's character, since her body has been found by the police during the first episode of season 1, leaving most characters and audiences a big puzzle, who is A. The old saying of "Three heads are better than one" is clearly not applied to *Pretty Little Liars*. As the story progresses, A obviously outwits the remaining four girls combined and their friends and family members. Four main roles include Aria, Emily, Hanna, and Spencer.

在《美少女的謊言》的第二季和第三季的萬聖節場景，可以說是全七季節目中最令人記憶深刻的。這也是了解艾莉森這個角色的一個很好的方式，既然她的遺體在第一季首集中被發現了，讓大多數的角色和許多觀眾遺留著一個很大的謎團，A 到底是誰呢？有句古老的俗諺說：「三個臭皮匠勝過一個諸葛亮」，但這顯然在《美少女的謊言》中並不適用。隨著故事的演進，A 顯然智勝僅存的四個女生，還有她們的朋友以及家庭成員。四個主要的角色包含了艾瑞亞、艾蜜莉、漢娜和史賓賽。

B. In season 2, before the disappearance of Allison,

there was a Halloween party that was hosted by Noel. All liars were anxious to find Allison, and they received a message from Allison, saying that she was in trouble. They eventually left the party and went to the empty macabre house. A search for Allison has begun, and they all held their breath while walking in a terrifying house. Eventually, they entered into a large room where there was no trace of Allison.

在第二季中，在艾莉森失蹤前，有個由諾爾所主辦的萬聖節派對。所有謊言成員們都熱切地在找尋艾莉森，然後他們收到了艾莉森的一則訊息，說道她正陷入麻煩中。她們最終離開了派對現場，前往恐怖的空置房間。找尋艾莉森的行動也就此展開了，而當走進令人感到恐怖的房子裡頭時，她們均屏氣凝神。最終，她們進入了一間大房間，但裡面沒有艾莉森的蹤跡。

C. Then the door unexpectedly closed and was locked. Thereafter, there came the voice of Allison. Allison was seen obviously struggling and fighting with someone outside the room. All girls could only see what was actually going on through the keyhole of the door knob. They swiftly thought of a way of using the smartphone to call 911.

接著，門出其不意地關上且鎖住了。在那之後，傳來了艾莉森的聲音。在門房外，艾莉森顯然與某個人在打鬥並掙扎著。所有女生們都僅能透過門把上的鑰匙孔觀看外面情況。她們很快地想到了使用智慧型手機撥打 911 求救。

D. However, there were no signals, so there was no way that they could get the help from the police. The scene made audiences' adrenalin rush heightened as Allison kept screaming. So did all liars. The guy was masked, so you cannot figure out the identity. The tension was dramatized as the time went by. Nevertheless, they soon figured that the open window was the way to get out of the house and see what actually happened here. After reentering the house, they found Allison who remained poised and unharmed on an armchair in the room, claiming that it was a mischief. As for the blood, her elucidation was that it was the ketchup. The identity of the costumed person was actually Noel.

然而，手機都沒有訊號，所以他們不可能得到警方的幫助。這個場景讓許多觀眾的腎上腺素飆升，當艾莉森持續發出驚叫。謊言成員們也是如此。這個男子戴上了面罩，所以你無法辨識出他的身分。隨著時間的流逝，緊張感也加劇了。儘管如此，她們馬上想到了開著的窗戶是離開這房子的唯一方法，並且能一睹到底實際上發生了什麼事情。在重新進到房內後，她們找到了艾莉森，其泰然自若且毫髮無傷地坐在房間內的扶手椅上，並稱剛才那齣是場玩笑。至於血的部分，她的解釋是那是番茄醬。面具裝扮者的身分實際上是諾爾。

E. All girls have been beguiled by Allison, and this is actually the type of the person that Allison is. When they all go back to the real party, Allison makes a gesture to Noel to thank him for portraying the role so that she gets to play the Halloween prank for the girls. Noel nervously explains to Allison that he does not go to the scary house because other things actually came up. The question remains, if Noel does not go to the house, then who, and this terrifies Allison as she begins to search for clues from the party. Apparently, there are multiple people wearing the mask. The real culprit can or cannot be here, and if this person is gunning for Allison or wants to hurt Allison, she does not have the chance to escape.

所有的女孩們都被艾莉森騙倒了，而實際上這就是艾莉森的本來的性格。當他們都回到真實的派對時，艾莉森對諾爾使個眼色，感謝他剛才扮演該角色，讓她能夠以萬聖節的鬧劇騙騙女孩們。諾爾緊張地向艾莉森解釋説，因為有事情耽擱了，所以他剛才沒辦法前往那間空屋。而問題仍舊存在著，如果諾爾沒有到那間房子裡，那麼那會是誰呢？想到這裡就讓艾莉森感到驚恐，當她從派對中掃視找尋線索時。顯然，有許多人都戴著面罩。真兇可能在此也可能並不在派對現場，而如果這個人真的在找尋機會或是想要傷害艾莉森，艾莉森絕沒有機會可逃。

F. Still Allison has plenty of actions that are questionable, and you might even wonder why she has to do things that way. Apparently, she needs help. There is also a scene where she is with her mother outside the coffee shop. They are congenial, enjoying the dessert and beverage. Then when Allison does not get what she wants, she stops breathing. Her mother disagrees with her having a party at the lake house. It is not until her mother screams "breathe" and agrees with her that she starts breathing. It is like she has been the problematic girl. No parents can handle her.

艾莉森仍有許多行徑是令人感到質疑的，而且你甚至可能會懷疑她為什麼有這樣的行為。顯然，她需要幫助。也有個場景是，艾莉森和她媽媽在咖啡店外頭。他們意氣相投，享用著甜點和飲料。然後，事情不如艾莉森意時，她停止呼吸。她媽媽不同意她在湖邊小屋辦派對。直到她母親驚喊「呼吸」並且表示同意後，她才開始呼吸。一直以來，她就是個問題女孩。沒有父母能夠應付得了她。

G. There are numerous questionable behaviors you will find throughout the series, including getting Jenna blind. There is a fire that unexpectedly starts by the girls during season 1.

在劇集中，還有為數眾多令人感到質疑的行為，包含致使簡納眼盲。在第一季中，女孩們出乎意料之外地引起了一場火災。

H. As for the real A, there are several clues in season 1 and season 3. If you have a keen eye for human relationships, you can easily identify those messages. Otherwise, you will be like multiple hornets following the hormone traces, but still cannot find the larder. That is also the writing strategies and narrations that want you to keep meandering and be loyal audiences that glue to the set.

而關於 A 的真實身分，在第一季和第三季都有幾個線索。如果你對於人的關係有著敏銳的察覺力，你就能夠輕而易舉地辨識出那些訊息。否則，你就像是循著賀爾蒙足跡的許多大黃蜂一樣，但是卻找不到巢穴所在。那也是寫作策略和敘述，讓你想要持續困在蜿蜒的小徑裡，黏著電視機，當個忠實的觀眾。

READING PASSAGE 2

You should spend about 20 minutes on **Questions 14-27**, which are based on Reading Passage 2 below.

Love Lesson:
How Bestsellers and Literature
Teach us to Love Smarter

A. As a saying goes, "preserve yourself from a first love, you need not fear a second." It is a good thought to think it that way if you are in a bad mood or if you are writing something poetic. In real life; however, we still need to find love, and yet cannot be too protective and be secluded. We just have to know the knack that makes us love smarter. Several classics have provided us a different thinking towards love, a preconception that can get us out of the trap. That is why those classics can endure the test of the time.

B. In *Gone with the Wind*, Scarlett's father, Gerald has provided his wisdom about love to Scarlett in an earlier chapter, when he senses something is going on between Scarlett's mind. He says "Have you been running after a man who's not in love with you, when you could have any of the bucks in the County?" and "Our people and the Wilkes are different." Still Scarlett does not know the nuances and cannot read between the lines, and she goes down the road of pursuing Ashley Wilkes. Even though she has many pursuers, Scarlett does not even know what love is. Scarlett does not have to go through the meandering route, if she knows what she wants and she knows what her father has said to her. Even Melanie knows better than she knows herself, so when there is a rumor between Scarlett and Ashley, Melanie knows Scarlett cannot have a feeling towards Ashley. If Scarlett had known herself, she wouldn't have made the statement "He never really existed at all, except in my imagination." at the very end of the fiction.

C. In *Wuthering Heights*, the main character Catherine also encounters the problem of love. After she has made the decision, Catherine goes to the housekeeper, Nelly Dean for help. Although Nelly may have been perceived as an incredible narrator, and so on, she can always be wise and see through the problem. Nelly does counter with a great question with Catherine's saying. When Catherine mentions two traits that most women use as the criteria for choosing their husband. Nelly cynically responds with a saying that "so that's enough for you? Just by being handsome and pleasant to be with, Linton can be your husband." Nelly nearly blurts out what surely opens my eyes.

D. You can sense the powerful message just by reading those simple sentences. Catherine eventually mentions the richness of Linton and plenty of things and attributes that make her love him. Nelly says "he won't always be handsome, and young, and may not be always rich." That is the most sagacious saying throughout the novel. Beauty unavoidably fades even with the plastic surgery's help. Time is more powerful than you. As to the wealth, no one can guarantee one's richness throughout the life, and there are always ups and downs in life. The question remains, why do you love Linton and want to be his wife? Even though she will be the bride who gets married with a handsome and rich guy, Catherine is still unhappy. The conversation is cynically accompanied by Nelly's words, "all seems smooth and easy, where is the obstacle?" Despite the fact that Catherine knows getting married with Linton is wrong, she has made the decision.

E. In *The Rule*, it does not include a wise bystander that inform you of the decision you are going to make, but it has listed 12 key rules for you to follow. You cannot gainsay that some notions are apparently old, but they do work. Nowadays, with technological improvements in electronic gadgets, everything has changed. You can easily get the message from others in an instant. Ironically, the speed date does not facilitate the time people who are currently finding their future life partners.

F. Most important of all, those devices do not make our love or marriage lasts. Even though we do not want to admit it, old wisdom and old saying actually triumph during the time. It is after all the psychology in human beings that we need to have a thorough understanding. After a long day's work, read these books and you will certainly find some useful ideas and avoid getting yourself fooled. Just like one of the rules, you can read some books, the reading time can prevent you from instantly replying one's messages. It will be good for a relationship in the long-term.

Questions 14-23

Look at the following statements (Questions 14-23) and the list of people below.

Match each statement with the correct people, A-G

Write the correct letter, A-G, in boxes 14-23 on your answer sheet.

NB You may use any letter more than once.

14 have a strong predilection towards someone despite the opposition

15 merely an illusion created by someone

16 one's expression contains acrimoniousness

17 aware of the subtle difference about one's brain

18 possess abundant qualities that are deemed the norm by many

19 one's unreliability recognized by many

20 similar dispositions are the key to a lasting relationship

21 possess the sagacity that can be consulted with

22 aware of the decision that is in conflict with inner voices

23 have doubts about the gossip

List of people

A Linton

B Gerald

C Catherine

D Nelly Dean

E Scarlett

F Melanie

G Ashley Wilkes

Questions 24-25

Do the following statements agree with the information given in the Reading Passage 2

In boxes 24-25 on your answer sheet, write

> **TRUE**- if the statement agrees with the information
>
> **FALSE**- if the statement contradicts the information
>
> **NOT GIVEN**- if there is no information on this

24. One should learn from the saying and be single throughout the lifetime.

25. Melanie uncovers the secret love affairs of Scarlett and Ashley, but chooses to be silent.

Questions 26-27

Complete the summary below

Choose No More Than One Word from the passage for each answer

Write your answers in boxes 26-27 on your answer sheet.

We are capable of getting out of the snare by adopting the advice given by those classics and books. Among them, *The Rule* has listed 12 important rules for readers to consider. Old notions are still able to endure the test of time, despite the fact that **26.**_____ have changed the way we find love. The development of the technology has been helpful, but there are limitations. There are things that we cannot control, such as **27.**_____ and lasting of wealth.

解析

08 ｜英國文學＋愛情

《Gone with the Wind》、《Wuthering Heights》和《The Rule》

經典文學和暢銷書教你愛得更聰明

　　在答題前第一個步驟是先快速掃視題目題型並快速制定答題策略，在這篇很快可以看到有配對題判斷題和摘要題，可以同步答這三類的題型。

◆ **第 24 題**，one should learn from the saying and be single throughout the lifetime 可以對應到第一段 As a saying goes, "preserve yourself from a first love, you need not fear a second." It is a good thought to think it that way if you are in a bad mood or if you are writing something poetic. In real life; however, we still need to find love, and yet cannot be too protective and be secluded. ，沒有説 be single 的部分，所以**要選 False**。

◆ **第 25 題**，Melanie uncovers the secret love affairs of Scarlett and Ashley, but chooses to be silent. ，這部分可以對應到 Even Melanie knows better than she knows herself, so when there is a rumor between Scarlett and Ashley, Melanie knows Scarlett cannot have a feeling towards Ashley. ，但是

沒有提到題目敘述的部分，故**答案為 Not Given**。（且在小說中自始自終她都不知道真相。）

◆ **第 14 題**，**14** have a strong predilection towards someone despite the opposition，可以對應到 He says "Have you been running after a man who's not in love with you, when you could have any of the bucks in the County?" and "Our people and the Wilkes are different." Still Scarlett does not know the nuances and read between the lines, and goes down the road of pursuing Ashley Wilkes.，儘管父親的反對和建議，她仍在追求 Ashley，故**答案為 E Scarlett**。

◆ **第 15 題**，**15** merely an illusion created by someone，對應到 If Scarlett had known herself, she wouldn't have made the statement "He never really existed at all, except in my imagination." at the very end of the fiction.由 Scarlett 創造出的幻想，**答案要選 G Ashley Wilkes**。

◆ **第 16 題**，**16** one's expression contains acrimoniousness，這點可以對應到 Nelly cynically responds with a saying that "so that's enough for you? Just by being handsome and pleasant to be with, Linton can be your husband." Nelly nearly blurts out what surely opens my eyes.，cynical 對應到 acrimoniousness，**答案要選 D Nelly Dean**。

◆ 第 **17** 題，**17** aware of the subtle difference about one's brain，這點可以對應到 n *Gone with the Wind*, Scarlett's father, Gerald has provided his wisdom about love to Scarlett in an earlier chapter, when he senses something is going on between Scarlett's mind.，他察覺出女兒怪怪的，似乎有內心事，答案要選 **B Gerald**。

◆ 第 **18** 題，**18** possess abundant qualities that are deemed the norm by many，這點可以對應到 When Catherine mentions two traits that most women use as the criteria for choosing their husband.，答案要選 **A Linton**。

◆ 第 **19** 題，**19** one's unreliability recognized by many，這點可以對應到 Although Nelly may have been perceived as an incredible narrator, and so on, she can always be wise and see through the problem.，答案要選 **D Nelly Dean**。

◆ 第 **20** 題，**20** similar dispositions are the key to a lasting relationship，這點可以對應到 He says "Have you been running after a man who's not in love with you, when you could have any of the bucks in the County?" and "Our people and the Wilkes are different."，答案要選 **B Gerald**。

◆ 第 **21** 題，**21** possess the sagacity that can be consulted with，這點可以對應到 After she has made the decision, Catherine goes to the housekeeper, Nelly Dean for help. Although Nelly may have been perceived as an incredible narrator, and so on, she can always be wise and see through the problem.，答案要選 **D Nelly Dean**。

◆ 第 **22** 題，**22** aware of the decision that is in conflict with inner voices，這點可以對應到 The conversation is cynically accompanied by Nelly's words, "all seems smooth and easy, where is the obstacle?" Despite the fact that Catherine knows getting married with Linton is wrong, she has made the decision.，答案要選 **C Catherine**。

◆ 第 **23** 題，**23** have doubts about the gossip，這點可以對應到 Even Melanie knows better than she knows herself, so when there is a rumor between Scarlett and Ashley, Melanie knows Scarlett cannot have a feeling towards Ashley.，答案要選 **F Melanie**。

◆ 第 **26** 和 **27** 題，答案分別為 **electronic gadgets** and **beauty**，第 26 題可以迅速定位回 E 段落找到答案，第 27 題則要理解 D 段落財富和美貌是不能持久的，然後選 beauty。

Test 3

MP3 020

TEST 1

TEST 2

TEST 3 Reading Passage 2

TEST 4

聽讀整合 TEST 3 P2

As a saying goes, "**1.**_____ yourself from a first love, you need not fear a second." It is a good thought to think it that way if you are in a bad mood or if you are writing something **2.**_____. In real life; however, we still need to find love, and yet cannot be too protective and be **3.**_____. We just have to know the **4.**_____ that makes us love smarter. Several classics have provided us a different thinking towards love, a **5.**_____ that can get us out of the trap. That is why those classics can endure the test of the time.

In *Gone with the Wind*, Scarlett's father, Gerald has provided his **6.**_____ about love to Scarlett in an earlier chapter, when he senses something is going on between Scarlett's mind.... and "Our people and the Wilkes are different." Still Scarlett does not know the **7.**_____ and cannot read between the **8.**_____, and she goes down the road of pursuing Ashley Wilkes. Even though she has many pursuers, Scarlett does not even know what love is. Scarlett does not have to go through the **9.**_____ route, if she knows what she wants and she knows what her father has said to her. Even Melanie knows better than she knows herself, so when there is a **10.**_____ between Scarlett and Ashley, Melanie knows Scarlett cannot have a feeling towards Ashley. If Scarlett had known herself, she wouldn't have made the statement "He never really existed at all, except in my **11.**_____." at the very end of the fiction.

In *Wuthering Heights*, the main character Catherine also encounters the problem of love. After she has made the decision, Catherine goes to the **12.**_____, Nelly Dean for help. Although Nelly may have been **13.**_____ as an incredible **14.**_____, and so on, she can always be wise and see through the problem. Nelly does counter with a great question with Catherine's saying. When Catherine mentions two traits that most women use as the **15.**_____ for choosing their husband. Nelly cynically responds with a saying that "so that's enough for you? Just by being **16.**_____ and **17.**_____ to be with, Linton can be your husband." Nelly nearly blurts out what surely opens my eyes.

You can sense the powerful message just by reading those simple sentences. Catherine eventually mentions the **18.**_____ of Linton and plenty of things and **19.**_____ that make her love him. Nelly says "he won't always be handsome, and young, and may not be always rich." That is the most **20.**_____ saying throughout the novel. Beauty **21.**_____ fades even with the **22.**_____ surgery's help. Time is more powerful than you. As to the **23.**_____, no one can guarantee one's richness throughout the life, and there are always ups and downs in life....The conversation is **24.**_____ accompanied by Nelly's words, "all seems smooth and easy, where is the **25.**_____?" Despite the fact that Catherine knows getting married with Linton is wrong, she has made the decision.

In *The Rule*, it does not include a wise **26.**_____ that inform you of the decision you are going to make, but it has listed 12 key rules for you to follow. You cannot gainsay that some notions are apparently old, but they do work. Nowadays, with **27.**_____ improvements in electronic **28.**_____, everything has changed. You can easily get the message from others in an instant. Ironically, the speed date does not **29.**_____ the time people who are currently finding their future life partners.

Most important of all, those devices do not make our love or **30.**_____ lasts. Even though we do not want to admit it, old wisdom and old saying actually triumph during the time. It is after all the **31.**_____ in human beings that we need to have a thorough **32.**_____. After a long day's work, read these books and you will certainly find some useful ideas and avoid getting yourself fooled...

A. As a saying goes, "preserve yourself from a first love, you need not fear a second." It is a good thought to think it that way if you are in a bad mood or if you are writing something poetic. In real life; however, we still need to find love, and yet cannot be too protective and be secluded. We just have to know the knack that makes us love smarter. Several classics have provided us a different thinking towards love, a preconception that can get us out of the trap. That is why those classics can endure the test of the time.

俗話說，「不要有初戀，你就不懼怕第二次的戀愛」。在你心情不好或是你正寫些具有詩意的話時，這樣思考是有益的。然而，在真實的生活中，我們仍舊需要找尋愛情，而無法過於保護自己或維持離群索居的生活。幾個經典鉅作提供了我們看待愛情不同的思考方向，先入為主的觀念能讓我們免於掉入陷阱。這也就是為什麼那些經典鉅作能夠經歷時間的考驗。

B. In *Gone with the Wind*, Scarlett's father, Gerald has provided his wisdom about love to Scarlett in an earlier chapter, when he senses something is going on between Scarlett's mind. He says "Have you been running after a man who's not in love with you, when

Test 3

1
TEST

2
TEST

3
TEST
Reading Passage 2

4
TEST

you could have any of the bucks in the County?" and "Our people and the Wilkes are different." Still Scarlett does not know the nuances and read between the lines, and goes down the road of pursuing Ashley Wilkes. Even though she has many pursuers, Scarlett does not even know what love is. Scarlett does not have to go through the meandering route, if she knows what she wants and she knows what her father has said to her. Even Melanie knows better than she knows herself, so when there is a rumor between Scarlett and Ashley, Melanie knows Scarlett cannot have a feeling towards Ashley. If Scarlett had known herself, she wouldn't have made the statement "He never really existed at all, except in my imagination." at the very end of the fiction.

在《亂世佳人》早先的章節中，思嘉莉的父親，傑拉爾德就提供了他對思嘉莉愛情的智慧之言，當他感受到思嘉莉的心理有著不尋常的念頭時。他說「妳一直追著不愛妳的男人跑，而妳實際上卻可以擁有郡裡任何一個男人？」而且「我們家族和威爾克斯家族是截然不同的」。思嘉莉仍舊察覺不出其中的細微差異並了解當中的言外之意，她繼續朝著追求艾希禮‧威爾克斯之路邁進。即使她有很多的追求者，思嘉莉仍舊不懂愛情是什麼。如果她能知道自己要什麼且了解她父親所對她說的話，那麼她就不用走那條崎嶇蜿蜒的路。甚至瑁蘭都比她更了解她自己，所以當思嘉莉和艾希禮之前傳出謠言時，瑨蘭知道思嘉莉對艾希禮是不可能有感情存在的。如果思嘉莉早點了解她自己的話，她就不會在小説結尾處做出「他完全未曾存在過，只存在我的想像世界裡頭」這樣的陳述。

C. In *Wuthering Heights*, the main character Catherine also encounters the problem of love. After she has made the decision, Catherine goes to the housekeeper, Nelly Dean for help. Although Nelly may have been perceived as an incredible narrator, and so on, she can always be wise and see through the problem. Nelly does counter with a great question with Catherine's saying. When Catherine mentions two traits that most women use as the criteria for choosing their husband. Nelly cynically responds with a saying that "so that's enough for you? Just by being handsome and pleasant to be with, Linton can be your husband." Nelly nearly blurts out what surely opens my eyes.

在《呼嘯山莊》，主角凱瑟琳也碰到愛情問題。在她已經做出決定後，凱瑟琳向管家奈利·狄恩尋求幫助。儘管奈利可能被認為是不可靠的敘述者，她總是機智過人且能看穿問題。對於凱瑟琳的提問奈利反問了一個很棒的問題。當凱瑟琳提到兩個特質，這是大多數女性都會用來當作挑選丈夫的特點。奈利冷嘲熱諷地回應「所以這樣對你來説就夠了嗎？

只要英俊而且人好相處，那林頓可以當你丈夫了」。奈利幾乎不經意說出口的話確實讓我眼界大開。

D. You can sense the powerful message just by reading those simple sentences. Catherine eventually mentions the richness of Linton and plenty of things and attributes that make her love him. Nelly says "he won't always be handsome, and young, and may not be always rich." That is the most sagacious saying throughout the novel. Beauty unavoidably fades even with the plastic surgery's help. Time is more powerful than you. As to the wealth, no one can guarantee one's richness throughout the life, and there are always ups and downs in life. The question remains, why do you love Linton and want to be his wife? Even though she will be the bride who gets married with a handsome and rich guy, Catherine is still unhappy. The conversation is cynically accompanied by Nelly's words, "all seems smooth and easy, where is the obstacle?" Despite the fact that Catherine knows getting married with Linton is wrong, she has made the decision.

藉由閱讀那些簡單的句子，你可以感受到其中存在強大的訊息。凱瑟琳最終提及林頓的富有以及許多事情和特質，這些都讓凱瑟琳愛上他。奈利則說「他不可能總是英俊、年輕且可能不會一直都那麼富裕」。那是整本小說中最睿智的哲言了。即使有著外科手術的幫助，美貌會無可避免地衰退。時間比你更強大。關於財富，沒有人可以保證自己終其一生都會富有，而人生中總是有起起落落。問題依舊，你到底因為什麼而愛林頓並願意當他的妻子呢？即使凱瑟琳終將成為一個既英俊又有錢的男人的妻子，她卻仍感到不快樂。對話緊接著伴隨著奈利的嘲諷，「看起來是那麼順利容易，那還有什麼困難呢？」儘管凱瑟琳知道嫁給林頓是錯的決定，她已下決定了。

E. In *The Rule*, it does not include a wise bystander that inform you of the decision you are going to make, but it has listed 12 key rules for you to follow. You cannot gainsay that some notions are apparently old, but they do work. Nowadays, with technological improvements in electronic gadgets, everything has changed. You can easily get the message from others in an instant. Ironically, the speed date does not facilitate the time people who are currently finding their future life partners.

在《戀愛必勝守則》，當中雖然沒有睿智的旁觀者來提醒你該如何下決定，但是卻列出了 12 條關鍵守則讓你遵循。你不能否認說那些觀念顯然過於老舊，但是它們確實奏效。現代，隨著電子裝置科技的進步，每件事情都已經有所改變了。你可以即刻從別人那裡獲得訊息。諷刺的是，快速約會並未讓人們現今找未來人生伴侶的時間有所加快。

F. Most important of all, those devices do not make our love or marriage lasts. Even though we do not want to admit it, old wisdom and old saying actually triumph during the time. It is after all the psychology in human beings that we need to have a thorough understanding. After a long day's work, read these books and you will certainly find some useful ideas and avoid yourself getting fooled. Just like one of the rules, you can read some books, the reading time can prevent you from instantly replying one's messages. It will be good for a relationship in the long-term.

最重要的是，那些裝置並不會讓我們的愛情或婚姻持久下去。即使我們不想承認，古老的智慧和俗諺確實在現下勝出。最後終究是需要我們對於人類心理有著透徹的了解才行。在一天長工時之後，閱讀這些書籍，而你確實會發現一些有用的想法，並且讓你不受到欺騙。就像是其中一條守則一樣，你可以閱讀一些書籍，閱讀的時間就能讓你免於即刻回覆別人訊息。這對於長期的感情關係來說是好事。

READING PASSAGE 3

You should spend about 20 minutes on **Questions 28-40**, which are based on Reading Passage 3 below.

Octopath Traveler: Misconceptions about Galdera the Fallen And the Game itself

A. The formidable final boss of the *Octopath Traveler*, Galdera the Fallen presents a tremendously huge challenge for most players. To defeat the final boss, proficiency in numerous skills and thorough knowledge of the game design are required. The final boss includes two phases. During the first phase, it consists of HP 500,000 that daunts most players, leading them to comment on that wall that "We have created the most difficult boss so far". The first phase of the final boss has a huge eyeball with numerous tentacles and they will get regenerated over time. Transmutation of its resistant to magic also changes during the combat.

B. The final boss of the second phase is even more challenging than that of the first.. The boss will be guarded by 99 impenetrable protection shields that make any attack ineffective unless the protection has been broken. The boss during this stage also has several appendages, but contrary to the tentacles of the first stage, they will not regrow. Apart from above-mentioned challenges, there are other things that will make gamers stagger along the way. The team's mobility will be immensely hamstrung by the final boss, making most players abdicate. Some have come up with ways by making even higher level, reaching an average of LV 85 to beat the boss, but it's a win by a nose. Research in *Octopath Traveler* has taken us to see the game in a different perspective.

C. For game designers, to reach extremely high LVs has never been their intentions. A quick glance in the statistics from the official game guide book can reveal the true story. Unless there are a huge difference in LV, say 20, figures of the character are quite close. Players have to think outside the box, instead of fixating on getting higher LVs. Further evidence from several videos solidifies the theory. With the same weapon for the team, players are able to defeat the boss with an average of LV 60-65, upending some players' viewpoints of beating the ultimate boss.

D. Without a complete understanding about the skills of each character, it's highly unlikely to triumph the ultimate boss. Some gamers have preconceived notions that certain characters are quite worthless, and that makes characters such as Scholar, take too much of the limelight. Since Scholar has much more appealing storyline, that makes it an even better pick. However, to beat the final boss requires a team effort, so players do need to be adept at operating all 8 characters and play equally well to win the game. The general thinking is that Hunter is useless, and there are other characters, like Hunter that have been misunderstood, but are quite worth taking a shot.

E. Take Hunter for example, it has **Leghold Trap** that can offer the team a few more rounds to initiate the powerful strike or to replenish the team with supply and get ready. **Leghold Trap** moves the boss action to the end, making the team pre-empt. Hunter also has a unique talent that is rarely used, but presents a powerful challenge for the boss. Hunter has a capture skill that can even apprehend the small boss from the side story or the maze. One particular boss can generate damage of 50,000 in a single hit to the first phrase of the final boss, one-tenth of the boss' HP. That can be the combined effort of all characters for a few more rounds.

F. Starseer, though having been often overlooked, has several skills that can turn the table. The final boss can initiate a magic cachet that immobilizes Sorcerer, making it unable to use the magic for three rounds. This can present a huge challenge for most players, since their strategy has been focusing on exportation of Sorcerer to generate the attack. Some even use the other three to assist the Sorcerer to accomplish the goal. Players who are well-acquainted with the skills of Starseer can easily use **Celestial Intervention** to remove enemy defuffs, the only way to remove the negative effect from the boss. Using Starseer as the secondary job to some characters is quite of help, and it has **Shooting Star** and **Steorra's Prophecy** that can do quite a damage to the boss if it is used properly.

G. Another thing is a lack of understanding about equipping the character with the right auxiliary skill. Several gamers are incapable of breaking the threshold and feel quite dumbfounded when they stumble upon other videos. Equipping with the same weapon, their attack is limited to 9999, while that of others are between 20,000 to 35,000. The key is to furnish the character with the correct auxiliary skill. Warrior's weapon skill, **Surpassing Power** is the solution. Each character with the **Surpassing Power** can generate the power over 9999, whether it is the physical attack or magic assault.

Questions 28-33

Complete the summary using the list of words and phrases A-R below

Write the correct letter, A-R in boxes 28-33 on your answer sheet.

Galdera the Fallen	DESCRIPTIONS
The first phase	• To take down the formidable boss, Galdera the Fallen, a high degree of skill and **28.**_____ about the game are necessary. • During the first phase, high **29.**_____ in HP discourages most players, earning the nickname "the most difficult boss so far". • **30.**_____ of numerous tentacles and its transmutation to magic make it even more challenging to tackle.

The second phase	◆ Attacks will be **31.**＿＿＿＿＿＿ due to palladium surrounded by the boss.
	◆ Gamers can still find themselves stagnated along the way. **32.**＿＿＿＿＿＿ of the final boss tremendously lower team's agility.
	◆ Some gamers have given up, while others have reached exceedingly high LVs to triumphantly conquer the boss.

Two professions	DESCRIPTIONS
Hunter	<ul><li>Hunter's **Leghold Trap** will give the team more time and **33.**_____ to get ready for the combat.</li><li>**Leghold Trap** even allows the team to preempt.</li><li>Capture skills are rarely used talents, but are in fact quite useful. **34.**_____ from labyrinths can generate a powerful hit, slashing one-tenth of the boss' HP.</li></ul>
Starseer	<ul><li>Sorcerer suffering from a magic cachet will remain **35.**_____.</li><li>This can present a huge challenge for most players.</li><li>However, the situation can be **36.**_____ by using Starseer's **Celestial Intervention**.</li></ul>

Boxes	
A protection	**B** challenge
C prepared	**D** replenishment
E seizure	**F** successful
G fruitless	**H** stature
I stationary	**J** unique
K volume	**L** erudition
M immobilize	**N** withdrawn
O shackles	**P** reconstruction
Q auxiliary	**R** effortless

Questions 37-40

Reading Passage 3 has SEVEN paragraphs, A-G

Which paragraph contains the following information?

Write the correct letter, A-G, in boxes 37-40 on your answer sheet.

NB You may use any letter more than once.

37 mention of a situation that regeneration will not occur

38 a description of a profession's supplementary skill that can help break the limit

39 mention of a profession that has gotten much attention

40 mention of a misconception that most gamers should evade

解析

09 ｜電玩遊戲＋學習
《*Octopath Traveler*》
八方旅人的遊戲攻略和破關要點

　　在答題前第一個步驟是先快速掃視題目題型並快速制定答題策略，在這篇很快可以看到配對題的部分，配對題大多是依順序出題，所以採取「**順答**」，照文章段落順序閱讀文章並答題。

◆ **第 28 題**，To take down the formidable boss, Galdera the Fallen, a high degree of skill and **28.**＿＿＿＿＿＿ about the game are necessary.，這部分可以對應到 To defeat the final boss, proficiency in numerous skills and thorough knowledge of the game design are required.，a high degree of skill 等於 **proficiency in numerous skills**，故要找能對應 knowledge 的同義字，掃描選項後可以看到 **L** erudition，故答案為 **L**。

◆ **第 29 題**，During the first phase, high **29.**＿＿＿＿＿＿ in HP discourages most players, earning the nickname "the most difficult boss so far".，這部分可以對應到 During the first phase, it consists of HP 500,000 that daunts most players, leading them to comment on that wall that "We have created the most difficult so far".，空格對應到 HP 500,000，

但是選項中沒有數字等關鍵字，出題者將 50 萬的血量改成了高血量，即 high volume in HP，故答案要選 **K**。

◆ 第 **30** 題，30.＿＿＿＿＿＿＿ of numerous tentacles and its transmutation to magic make it even more challenging to tackle.，這部分可以對應到 The first phase of the final boss has a huge eyeball with numerous tentacles and they will get regenerated over time. Transmutation of its resistant to magic also changes during the combat.對應到的訊息點是 will get regenerate，所以要找 regenerate 的同義字且是名詞的形式，在選項中可以找到 **P** reconstruction，故答案要選 **P**。

◆ 第 **31** 題，Attacks will be **31.**＿＿＿＿＿＿＿ due to palladium surrounded by the boss.，這部分可以對應到 The boss is guarded by 99 impenetrable protection shields that make any attack ineffective unless the protection is broken.，palladium 對應到 protection shields，空格處對應到 ineffective，故要選 **G** fruitless，答案為 **G**。

◆ 第 **32** 題，Gamers can still find themselves stagnated along the way, **32.**＿＿＿＿＿＿ of the final boss tremendously lower team's agility.，這部分可以對應到 Apart from above-mentioned challenges, there are other things that will make gamers stagger along the way. The team's mobility will be immensely hamstrung by the final boss, making most players abdicate. ，當中 stagnated 對應到 stagger，而 agility 對應到 mobility，hamstrung 對應到空格處，指的是束縛，對應到選項 O 桎梏、束縛，故答案要選 **O** shackles。

◆ **第 33 題**，Hunter's **Leghold Trap** will give the team more time and **33.**＿＿＿＿＿ to get ready for the combat. ，這部分可以對應到 Take Hunter for example, it has **Leghold Trap** that can offer the team a few more rounds to initiate the powerful strike or to replenish the team with supply and get ready. ，當中 get ready 對應到 time 而 replenish the team with supply 指的是補給，剛好可以對應到 **D** replenishment，故**答案要選 D**。

◆ **第 34 題**，Capture skills are rarely used talents, but are in fact quite useful. **34.**＿＿＿＿＿ from labyrinths can generate a powerful hit, slashing one-tenth of the boss' HP. ，這部分可以對應到 Hunter also has a unique talent that is rarely used, but presents a powerful challenge for the boss. Hunter has a capture skill that can even apprehend the small boss from the side story or the maze. ，當中 maze 對應到 labyrinth，空格處對應到 apprehend，故要找選項中符合的同義字，**E** seizure，**答案要選 E**。

◆ **第 35 題**，Sorcerer suffering from a magic cachet will remain **35.＿＿＿＿＿** . ，這部分可以對應到 The final boss can initiate a magic cachet that immobilize Sorcerer, making it unable to use the magic for three rounds.要選跟 immobilize 的同義字，但是要根據語法要選**形容詞**，**I** stationary，故**要選 I**。

◆ **第 36 題**，However, the situation can be **36.＿＿＿＿＿** by using Starseer's **Celestial Intervention**. ，這部分可以對應到 Players who are well-acquainted with the skills of Starseer can easily use **Celestial Intervention** to remove enemy defuffs, the only way to remove the negative effect from the boss. ，空格處對應到 remove，要選 remove 的同義詞且是形容詞，**N withdrawn** 符合，故**答案要選 N**。

◆ **第 37 題**，**37** mention of a situation that regeneration will not occur，這題要對應到 The boss during this stage also has several appendages, but contrary to the tentacles of the first stage, they will not regrow，觸手在第二階段時不會增生，故**答案要選 B**。

◆ **第 38 題**，**38** a description of a profession's supplementary skill that can help break the limit，這題要對應到 Warrior's weapon skill, **Surpassing Power** is the solution. Each character with the **Surpassing Power** can generate the power over 9999, whether it is the physical attack or magic assault.，故答案要選 **G**。

• 第 **39** 題，**39** mention of a profession that has gotten much attention，這題要對應到 Some gamers have preconceived notions that certain characters are quite worthless, and that makes characters such as Scholar, take too much of the limelight.，學者已經獲得太多的關注了，故答案要選 **D**。

• 第 **40** 題，**40** mention of a misconception that most gamers should evade，Players have to think outside the box, instead of fixating on getting higher LVs. Further evidence from several videos solidifies the theory. With the same weapon for the team, players are able to defeat the boss with an average of LV 60-65, upending some players' viewpoints of beating the ultimate boss.，高等級並非成功挑戰王的解方，也非官方遊戲設計的目的，故**答案要選 C**。

The **1.**_____ final boss of the *Octopath Traveler*, Galdera the Fallen presents a **2.**_____ huge challenge for most players. To defeat the final boss, **3.**_____ in numerous skills and thorough knowledge of the game design are required. The final boss includes two phases. During the first phase, it consists of HP 500,000 that **4.**_____ most players, leading them to comment on that wall that "We have created the most difficult boss so far". The first phase of the final boss has a huge **5.**_____ with numerous **6.**_____ and they will get **7.**_____ over time. **8.**_____ of its resistant to magic also changes during the combat. The final boss of the second phase is even more challenging than that of the first. The boss will be **9.**_____ by 99 **10.**_____ protection shields that make any attack **11.**_____ unless the protection has been broken. The boss during this stage also has several **12.**_____, but contrary to the tentacles of the first stage, they will not **13.**_____. Apart from above-mentioned challenges, there are other things that will make gamers **14.**_____ along the way. The team's **15.**_____ will be immensely **16.**_____ by the final boss, making most players abdicate. Some have come up with ways by making even higher level, reaching an average of LV 85 to beat the boss, but it's a win by a nose...

For game designers, to reach extremely high LVs has never been their intentions. A quick glance in the **17.**_____ from the official game guide book can reveal the true story. Unless there are a huge **18.**_____ in LV, say 20, figures of the character are quite close. Players have to think outside the box, instead of **19.**_____ on getting higher LVs. Further evidence from several videos solidifies the theory. With the same **20.**_____ for the team, players are able to defeat the boss with an average of LV 60-65, upending some players' viewpoints of beating the ultimate boss.

Without a complete understanding about the skills of each character, it's highly unlikely to **21.**_____ the ultimate boss. Some gamers have preconceived notions that certain characters are quite worthless, and that makes characters such as Scholar, take too much of the **22.**_____. Since Scholar has much more appealing storyline, that makes it an even better pick. However, to beat the final boss requires a team effort, so players do need to be adept at operating all 8 characters and play equally well to win the game....

Take Hunter for example, it has **Leghold Trap** that can offer the team a few more rounds to **23.**_____ the powerful strike or to **24.**_____ the team with supply and get ready. **Leghold Trap** moves the boss action to the end, making the team pre-empt. Hunter also has a unique talent that is rarely used, but presents a powerful challenge for the boss. Hunter has a capture skill that can even **25.**_____ the small boss from the side story or the maze. One particular boss can **26.**_____ damage of 50,000 in a single hit to the first phrase of the final boss, one-tenth of the boss' HP....

Starseer, though having been often overlooked, has several skills

that can turn the table. The final boss can initiate a magic **27.**_____
_____ that **28.**_____ Sorcerer, making it unable to use
the magic for three rounds. This can present a huge challenge for
most players, since their strategy has been focusing on **29.**_____
_____ of Sorcerer to generate the attack. Some even use the
other three to assist the Sorcerer to accomplish the goal. Players
who are well-acquainted with the skills of Starseer can easily use
Celestial Intervention to remove enemy defuffs, the only way to
remove the negative effect from the boss. Using Starseer as the
30._____ job to some characters is quite of help, and it
has **Shooting Star** and **Steorra's Prophecy** that can do quite a
damage to the boss if it is used properly. Another thing is a lack
of understanding about equipping the character with the right
31._____ skill. Several gamers are incapable of breaking
the threshold and feel quite **32.**_____ when they stumble
upon other videos. Equipping with the same weapon, their attack
is limited to 9999, while that of others are between 20,000 to
35,000. The key is to furnish the character with the correct
auxiliary skill. Warrior's weapon skill, **Surpassing Power** is the
solution....

中譯和影子跟讀   MP3 021

A. The formidable final boss of the *Octopath Traveler*, Galdera the Fallen presents a tremendously huge challenge for most players. To defeat the final boss, proficiency in numerous skills and thorough knowledge of the game design are required. The final boss includes two phases. During the first phase, it consists of HP 500,000 that daunts most players, leading them to comment on that wall that "We have created the most difficult boss so far". The first phase of the final boss has a huge eyeball with numerous tentacles and they will get regenerated over time. Transmutation of its resistant to magic also changes during the combat.

《八方旅人》難以對付的最終魔王傑拉爾德對大多數遊戲玩家造成了極大的挑戰。要擊敗最終魔王，精通為數眾多的技能和透徹地掌握遊戲設計內所含的知識是必須的。最終魔王包含了兩個階段。在第一個階段，最終魔王具有 50 萬的血量，光此就讓大多數玩家心生畏懼，導致他們在牆上留言說道「我們創造了目前為止最難挑戰的魔王了」。第一階段的魔王有著巨大的眼球，附有許多觸手，且觸手會隨著時間增生。在戰鬥期間，其本身對魔法的抗性亦會隨之產生變化。

B. The final boss of the second phase is even more challenging than that of the first. The boss will be guarded by 99 impenetrable protection shields that make any attack ineffective unless the protection has been broken. The boss during this stage also has several appendages, but contrary to the tentacles of the first stage, they will not regrow. Apart from above-mentioned challenges, there are other things that will make gamers stagger along the way. The team's mobility will be immensely hamstrung by the final boss, making most players abdicate. Some have come up with ways by making even higher level, reaching an average of LV 85 to beat the boss, but it's a win by a nose. Research in *Octopath Traveler* has taken us to see the game in a different perspective.

第二個階段的最終魔王甚至比起第一階段的魔王更具挑戰性。除非破盾，第二個階段的魔王具有無法穿透的 99 道保護盾，能讓任何攻擊無效。此階段的魔王也有著幾個附屬肢體，但是與第一階段的觸手相比，牠們不會重生。除了上述所提到的挑戰之外，尚有其他的挑戰會讓玩家們在打王的過程中步履蹣跚。團隊的機動性會受到最終魔王極大的束縛，讓大多數玩家放棄打王。有些玩家甚至想出了方法，即獲取更高的等級，達到平均等級 85 級以擊敗最終魔王，但是卻僅是以些微差距險勝。《八方旅人》的研究引領我們以不同的角度來看待這款遊戲。

C. For game designers, to reach extremely high LVs has never been their intentions. A quick glance in the statistics from the official game guide book can reveal the true story. Unless there are a huge difference in LV, say 20, figures of the character are quite close. Players have to think outside the box, instead of fixating on getting higher LVs. Further evidence from several videos solidifies the theory. With the same weapon for the team, players are able to defeat the boss with an average of LV 60-65, upending some players' viewpoints of beating the ultimate boss.

對遊戲設計師來說，達到極高的等級一直都不是他們的設計初衷。很快地從官方攻略本的統計一瞥就能看出真相。除非之間有著像是 20 級的等級差距，角色的數值是相當接近的。玩家們必須要跳脫框架思考，而非執著於獲取更高的等級。從幾個視頻中更能找到進一步的證據以鞏固此論述。彼此有著相同武器，玩家們能夠在平均等級 60 至 65 就能夠擊敗最終魔王。

D. Without a complete understanding about the skills of each character, it's highly unlikely to triumph the ultimate boss. Some gamers have preconceived notions that certain characters are quite worthless, and that makes characters such as Scholar, take too much of the limelight. Since Scholar has much more appealing storyline, that makes it an even better pick. However, to beat the final boss requires a team effort, so players do need to be adept at operating all 8 characters and play equally well to win the game. The general thinking is that Hunter is useless, and there are other characters, like Hunter that have been misunderstood, but are quite worth taking a shot.

對每個角色的技能缺乏完整的掌握是很難戰勝最終魔王的。有些玩家對於特定的角色有著先入為主的概念，認為他們不具有價值，而這也讓有些角色，例如學者成了許多人眾所矚目的焦點。既然學者有較具吸引人的故事主線，這讓其成了更好的選擇。然而，要打敗最終魔王需要團隊的努力，玩家們確實需要對所有八個角色的操作都擅長且都玩得很好才能贏得勝利。玩家們普遍覺得獵人的角色是無用的，而像是獵人這樣的角色是一直受到誤解的，但其卻相當值得一試的。

E. Take Hunter for example, it has **Leghold Trap** that can offer the team a few more rounds to initiate the powerful strike or to replenish the team with supply and get ready. **Leghold Trap** moves the boss action to the end, making the team pre-empt. Hunter also has a unique talent that is rarely used, but presents a powerful challenge for the boss. Hunter has a capture skill that can even apprehend the small boss from the side story or the maze. One particular boss can generate damage of 50,000 in a single hit to the first phrase of the final boss, one-tenth of the boss' HP. That can be the combined effort of all characters for a few more rounds.

以獵人為例，他具有「黏著補網」這項技能，能讓團隊有更多回合發起強大的攻擊或是補充團隊的補給且準備就緒。「黏著補網」會使魔王的行動被移置最後，讓團隊能夠先發制人。獵人也還有一項獨特的技能，卻鮮少被使用到，其能對魔王產生強大的挑戰。獵人具有捕獲技能，甚至能夠捕獲支線故事和野外迷宮的小王。其中一個特定的小王就能在一次攻擊中，對第一階段的最終魔王產生 5 萬的傷害值，是魔王血量的 1/10。那是所有角色好幾回合共同合力攻擊的傷害數值。

F. Starseer, though having been often overlooked, has several skills that can turn the table. The final boss can initiate a magic cachet that immobilizes Sorcerer, making it unable to use the magic for three rounds. This can present a huge challenge for most players, since their strategy has been focusing on exportation of Sorcerer to generate the attack. Some even use the other three to assist the Sorcerer to accomplish the goal. Players who are well-acquainted with the skills of Starseer can easily use **Celestial Intervention** to remove enemy defuffs, the only way to remove the negative effect from the boss. Using Starseer as the secondary job to some characters is quite of help, and it has **Shooting Star** and **Steorra's Prophecy** that can do quite a damage to the boss if it is used properly.

儘管通常一直受到忽視，占星師也有幾項技能可以扭轉局勢。最終魔王能對魔術師發起魔法封印，使其無法行動，讓魔術師三回合無法使用魔法。此舉對於大多數玩家產生了極大的挑戰，因為他們的策略是仰賴魔術師的輸出以產生攻擊。有些玩家甚至使用其他三個角色來輔助魔術師以達到攻略最終魔王的目的。對占星師的技能瞭若指掌的玩家就能輕易使用「天國的調停/煙消雲散」移除敵方施加的弱化能力，唯一一個能夠移除魔王所施加的負面效果。有些角色使用占星師當作副職業是相當有幫助的，且占星師具有「流星」和「史黛歐拉的預言」，如果使用得當的話，能對魔王產生相當大的傷害。

G. Another thing is a lack of understanding about equipping the character with the right auxiliary skill. Several gamers are incapable of breaking the threshold and feel quite dumbfounded when they stumble upon other videos. Equipping with the same weapon, their attack is limited to 9999, while that of others are between 20,000 to 35,000. The key is to furnish the character with the correct auxiliary skill. Warrior's weapon skill, **Surpassing Power** is the solution. Each character with the **Surpassing Power** can generate the power over 9999, whether it is the physical attack or magic assault.

另一項重點是,缺乏了將角色配上對的輔助技能的了解。有幾個玩家就無法突破門檻,而對此感到困惑,直到偶然看到其他視頻才恍然大悟。具備同樣的武器,他們的攻擊數值受限於 9999,而其他玩家卻能造成 2 萬到 3 萬 5 的傷害值。關鍵就在於,角色裝備了正確的輔助技能。武藝家的武器技能,「突破能力界限」就是解方。不論是物理攻擊還是魔法攻擊,每位裝備「突破能力界限」的角色都能產生超過 9999 的攻擊數值。

Test 3

Reading passage 1 (1-13)

1. D
2. D
3. F
4. F
5. G
6. C
7. B
8. False
9. True
10. keyhole
11. smartphone
12. masked
13. poised

Reading passage 2 (14-27)

14. E
15. G
16. D
17. B
18. A
19. D
20. B
21. D
22. C
23. F
24. False
25. Not Given
26. electronic gadgets
27. beauty

Reading passage 3 (28-40)

28. L
29. K
30. P
31. G
32. O
33. D
34. E
35. I
36. N
37. B
38. G
39. D
40. C

聽讀整合　參考答案

Test 3 P1

1. Halloween
2. puzzle
3. outwits
4. members
5. disappearance
6. anxious
7. message
8. macabre
9. terrifying
10. trace
11. voice
12. obviously
13. keyhole
14. swiftly
15. smartphone
16. signals
17. adrenalin
18. heightened
19. identity
20. dramatized
21. window
22. poised
23. armchair
24. mischief
25. elucidation
26. ketchup
27. portraying
28. clues
29. coffee
30. congenial
31. blind
32. hormone

Test 3 P2

1. preserve
2. poetic
3. secluded
4. knack
5. preconception
6. wisdom
7. nuances
8. lines
9. meandering
10. rumor
11. imagination
12. housekeeper
13. perceived
14. narrator
15. criteria
16. handsome
17. pleasant
18. richness
19. attributes
20. sagacious
21. unavoidably
22. plastic
23. wealth
24. cynically
25. obstacle
26. bystander
27. technological
28. gadgets
29. facilitate
30. marriage
31. psychology
32. understanding

Test 3 P2

1. formidable
2. tremendously
3. proficiency
4. daunts
5. eyeball
6. tentacles
7. regenerated
8. Transmutation
9. guarded
10. impenetrable
11. ineffective
12. appendages
13. regrow
14. stagger
15. mobility
16. hamstrung
17. statistics
18. difference
19. fixating
20. weapon
21. triumph
22. limelight
23. initiate
24. replenish
25. apprehend
26. generate
27. cachet
28. immobilize
29. exportation
30. secondary
31. auxiliary
32. dumbfounded

Test 4

篇章概述

10

有錢人跟你想的不一樣❷

在這篇很快可以看到配對題搭摘要題，算是蠻好攻略的搭配，可以順著讀先答配對題。

11

一個動人的偉大愛情故事

在答題前第一個步驟是先快速掃視題目題型並快速制定答題策略，在這篇很快可以看到完成句子配對題和摘要式填空，可以一併回答或者是先答摘要式填空。

12

探究為什麼實境秀選出來的冠、亞軍，在賽後卻無法長紅

在這篇很快可以看到段落標題試題和摘要題，可以先寫段落標題邊順讀答題，最後攻略摘要題。

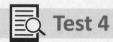

READING PASSAGE 1
You should spend about 20 minutes on **Questions 1-13**, which are based on Reading Passage 1 below.

Business School Cases:
Secrets of the Millionaire Mind ❷

A. Imagine a world in which getting married with a male millionaire were confined to females who are very pretty. Before long, people would assume that being a bombshell will be destined to the gateway to be wealthy. Obviously, possessing outer beauty is not enough even though that will help beautiful people get closer to the dream. Yet there are other things to consider. Research in wealth and secrets of the millionaire mind will help you look closer at what is in the mind of those millionaires.

B. Although people are reluctant to admit the fact that luck does play a key role in determining how one gets picked by a millionaire, luck is surely more important than other factors, such as diploma and appearances. In *Match Point*, Nola is an overly attractive knockout, but Tom's mother has obviously not been a big fan of her, which makes her way to the marriage faltering and stagnated. During the conversation with his friend Chris, Tom confides that "It's taken mother a while to get used to the idea that I'm serious about her. Mother's always had this funny little agenda for me which doesn't involve marrying a struggling actress." At a much later time, Nola is constantly being questioned by Tom's mother Eleanor. The innuendos include "It's a particular cruel business for a woman and as you get older and time passes if nothing happens it gets harder and harder. But I am a great one for facing up to realities." Of course, the chat goes unpleasant for both parties as Tom raises the voice to his mother. Chris, on the other hand, has been getting the preference for Tom's parents that leads to a completely different outcome. Chris even gets married with Tom's sister.

C. The luck theory of getting liked by the millionaire's parents can be further proved by several storylines in *Desperate Housewives*. After the ending of the first marriage, Gaby is pursued by Victor, who is extremely wealthy. Gaby seems to know every Victor's move and outmaneuvers him on the surface, but what she has failed to notice is that Victor is using her to get more votes for certain groups. She learns the news on her wedding day by inadvertently overhearing the conversation between Victor and his father. Beforehand, his father skillfully saves the couple's quarreling over something trivial. Then again in a later time, when Gaby leaves a telephone message, saying that she is leaving him. Victor's father once again beguiles

Gaby by saying she can freely add zeros on the check, if she leaves Victor after the election. The manipulation works. It is not until Victor's funeral does Gaby realize that the money is all in Victor's father name, and Victor has no money. Gaby cannot clinch her father-in-law.

D.   In *Desperate Housewives*, luck does work in Susan's favor when she starts the relationship with the multi-millionaire, Ian. Ian is incredibly rich with a castle, but like what's in Gaby's case and Nola's situation, the groom's parents are the key to a successful marriage. The marriage cannot even have a start if there is a veto from Ian's parents. The meeting with Ian's parents goes well until Susan makes a comment that raises a red flag for Ian's mother. Later, Ian's mother has a serious talk with them both, saying that if she eventually gets a divorce with Ian, she will accept a cash settlement and not go after the property and the castile Ian inherits from them. Even though Susan comes up with other way to avoid signing the pre-nuptial agreement, her relationship with Ian does not work out.

E.   Aside from getting liked by the parents of the millionaire, what most people don't know is the fact that rich people are unwilling to give the company's stock to their spouse. This can be verified in both *Revenge* and *Grinding it out*. In *Revenge*, Victoria is smart and competent, but during the divorce, her ex-husband makes an excuse of saying he doesn't want to let his father down. He can only give Victoria the house, the deed of the Grayson Manor, even if Victoria asks him about the shares of the company. *Grinding it out* shares a similar vein. Ray doesn't want to give the shares of McDonald to his first wife because that's too valuable. He is only willing to give his first wife something tangible, such as the house.

Questions 11-13

Complete the summary below

Choose No More Than One Word from the passage for each answer

Write your answers in boxes 11-13 on your answer sheet.

A conclusion can be drawn that the method of getting married with the rich is by being a **11.**_____. However, a closer look can reveal that diploma and **12.**_____ are not the determinant. Luck, on the other hand, is more important, as can be seen in the case of *Match Point*. Tom's mother makes several statements about Nola's career. One includes the fact that it is a ruthless path for women, **13.**_____ and time can also be cruel factors.

Questions 1-10

Look at the following statements (Questions 1-10) and the list of people below.

Match each statement with the correct people, A-M

Write the correct letter, A-M, in boxes 1- on your answer sheet.

NB You may use any letter more than once.

1 has a profession that is obviously faltering

2 outsmarts someone in many circumstances

3 surreptitiously has another agenda

4 salvages a skirmish between two people

5 negotiates a deal between two people

6 uses disappointment as an excuse

7 is in fact an empty shell on the surface

8 makes an allusive remark to disparage someone

9 gets the preferential treatment from some people

10 uses deception that actually beguiles someone

List of people

A Gaby

B Victor

C Nola

D Ian's mother

E Susan

F Gaby's father-in-law

G Chris

H Tom's parents

I Eleanor

J Victoria

K Ray

L Victor

M Victoria's ex-husband

解析

10｜商管＋心靈成長

《*Grinding it out*》、《*Revenge*》、《慾望師奶》和《*Match Point*》

有錢人跟你想的不一樣❷

　　在答題前第一個步驟是先快速掃視題目題型並快速制定答題策略，在這篇很快可以看到配對題搭摘要題，算是蠻好攻略的搭配，可以順著讀先答配對題。

◆ **第 1 題**，1 has a profession that is obviously faltering，這部分可以對應到 During the conversation with his friend Chris, Tom confides that "It's taken mother a while to get used to the idea that I'm serious about her. Mother's always had this funny little agenda for me which doesn't involve marrying a struggling actress."，所以指的是 Nola，**答案為 C Nola**。

◆ **第 2 題**，2 outsmarts someone in many circumstances，這部分可以對應到 Gaby seems to **know every Victor's move and outmaneuvers him on the surface**, but what she has failed to notice is that Victor is using her to get more votes for certain groups.，所以指的是 Gaby，**答案為 A Gaby**。

◆ **第 3 題**，**3** surreptitiously has another agenda，這部分可以對應到 Gaby seems to know every Victor's move and outmaneuvers him on the surface, but what she has failed to notice is that Victor is using her to get more votes for certain groups.，所以指的是 Victor，答案為 **B Victor**。

◆ **第 4 題**，**4** salvages a skirmish between two people，這部分可以對應到 Beforehand, his father skillfully saves the couple's quarreling over something trivial.，所以指的是 Gaby's father-in-law，答案為 **F Gaby's father-in-law**。

◆ **第 5 題**，**5** negotiates a deal between two people，這部分可以對應到 Later, Ian's mother has a serious talk with them both, saying that if she eventually gets a divorce with Ian, she will accept a cash settlement not go after the property and the castile Ian inherits from them.，所以指的是 Ian's mother，答案為 **D Ian's mother**。

◆ **第 6 題**，**6** uses disappointment as an excuse，這部分可以對應到 In *Revenge*, Victoria is smart and competent, but during the divorce, her ex-husband makes an excuse of saying he doesn't want to let his father down.，所以指的是 Victoria's ex-husband，答案為 **M Victoria's ex-husband**。

◆ 第 7 題，**7** is in fact an empty shell on the surface，這部分可以對應到 The manipulation works. It is not until Victor's funeral does Gaby realizes that the money is all in Victor's father name, and Victor has no money. Gaby cannot clinch her father-in-law.，所以指的是 Victor，**答案為 B Victor**。

◆ 第 8 題，**8** makes an allusive remark to disparage someone，這部分可以對應到 The innuendos include "It's a particular cruel business for a woman and as you get older and time passes if nothing happens it gets harder and harder. But I am a great one for facing up to realities."，所以指的是 **Eleanor**，**答案為 I Eleanor**。

◆ 第 9 題，**9** gets the preferential treatment from some people，這部分可以對應到 Chris, on the other hand, gets the preference from Tom's parents that leads to a completely different outcome. Chris even gets married with Tom's sister.，所以指的是 Chris，**答案為 G Chris**。

◆ 第 10 題，**10** uses deception that actually beguiles someone，這部分可以對應到 Victor's father once again beguiles Gaby by saying she can freely add zeros on the check, if she leaves Victor after the election. The manipulation works. 所以指的是 Gaby's father-in-law，**答案**

為 **F Gaby's father-in-law**。

◆ **第 11 題**，A conclusion can be drawn that the method of getting married with the rich is by being a **11.**_____. ，這部分可以對應到 Imagine a world in which getting married with a male millionaire were confined to females who are very pretty. Before long, people would assume that being a **bombshell** will be destined to the gateway to be wealthy.，故答案為 **bombshell**。

◆ **第 12 題**，However, a closer look can reveal that diploma and **12.**_____ are not the determinant. Luck, on the other hand, is more important, as can be seen in the case of *Match Point*.，這部分可以對應到 Although people are reluctant to admit the fact that luck does play a key role in determining how one gets picked by a millionaire, luck is surely more important than other factors, such as diploma and appearances.，故答案為 **appearances**。

◆ **第 13 題**，Tom's mother makes several statements about Nola's career. One includes the fact that it is a ruthless path for women, **13.**_____ and time can also be cruel factors.，這部分可以對應到 "It's a particular cruel business for a woman and as you get older and time passes if nothing happens it gets harder and harder. But I am a great one for facing up to realities.",這題的答案較隱晦,但可以由 get older 反推出老化或歲月流逝,故**答案為 aging**。

Imagine a world in which getting married with a male **1.**_____
____ were confined to females who are very pretty. Before long,
people would **2.**_____ that being a **3.**_____ will be
destined to the gateway to be wealthy. Obviously, possessing **4.**__
_____ beauty is not enough even though that will help
beautiful people get closer to the dream....

Although people are **5.**_____ to admit the fact that luck
does play a key role in **6.**_____ how one gets picked by a
millionaire, luck is surely more important than other factors, such
as **7.**_____ and appearances. In *Match Point*, Nola is an
overly attractive **8.**_____, but Tom's mother has obviously
not been a big fan of her, which makes her way to the marriage
faltering and **9.**_____. During the conversation with his
friend Chris, Tom confides that "It's taken mother a while to get
used to the idea that I'm serious about her. Mother's always had
this funny little **10.**_____ for me which doesn't involve
marrying a **11.**_____ actress." ...The **12.**_____
include "It's a particular cruel business for a woman and as you
get older and time passes if nothing happens it gets harder and
harder. But I am a great one for facing up to **13.**_____." Of
course, the chat goes **14.**_____ for both parties as Tom
raises the voice to his mother. Chris, on the other hand, has been
getting the **15.**_____ for Tom's parents that leads to a
completely different outcome. Chris even gets married with
Tom's sister.

...After the ending of the first marriage, Gaby is pursued by Victor, who is extremely **16.**_____. Gaby seems to know every Victor's move and **17.**_____ him on the surface, but what she has failed to notice is that Victor is using her to get more votes for certain groups. She learns the news on her wedding day by **18.**_____ overhearing the conversation between Victor and his father. Beforehand, his father **19.**_____ saves the couple's quarreling over something **20.**_____. Then again in a later time, when Gaby leaves a telephone message, saying that she is leaving him. Victor's father once again beguiles Gaby by saying she can freely add **21.**_____ on the check, if she leaves Victor after the **22.**_____.

The **23.**_____ works. It is not until Victor's funeral does Gaby realize that the money is all in Victor's father name, and Victor has no money. Gaby cannot **24.**_____ her father-in-law.

In *Desperate Housewives*, luck does work in Susan's favor when she starts the relationship with the multi-millionaire, Ian. Ian is incredibly rich with a **25.**_____, but like what's in Gaby's case and Nola's situation, the groom's parents are the key to a successful marriage. The marriage cannot even have a start if there is a **26.**_____ from Ian's parents....Later, Ian's mother has a serious talk with them both, saying that if she eventually gets a **27.**_____ with Ian, she will accept a cash **28.**_____ and not go after the property and the castle Ian inherits from them. Even though Susan comes up with other way to avoid signing the **29.**_____ agreement, her relationship with Ian does not work out.

Aside from getting liked by the parents of the millionaire, what most people don't know is the fact that rich people are unwilling to give the company's **30.**_____ to their spouse.... In *Revenge*, Victoria is smart and competent, but during the divorce, her ex-husband makes an excuse of saying he doesn't want to let his father down. He can only give Victoria the house, the **31.**_____ of the Grayson Manor, even if Victoria asks him about the shares of the company. *Grinding it out* shares a similar vein. Ray doesn't want to give the shares of McDonald to his first wife because that's too valuable. He is only willing to give his first wife something **32.**_____, such as the house.

中譯和影子跟讀 MP3 022

A. Imagine a world in which getting married with a male millionaire were confined to females who are very pretty. Before long, people would assume that being a bombshell will be destined to the gateway to be wealthy. Obviously, possessing outer beauty is not enough even though that will help beautiful people get closer to the dream. Yet there are other things to consider. Research in wealth and secrets of the millionaire mind will help you look closer at what is in the mind of those millionaires.

想像居住在一個世界裡，與男性百萬富翁們結婚的女性對象都僅限於具有沉魚落雁之姿的女性。不久之後，人們就會假定一個花容月貌的女子注定就是通往財富的途徑。顯然，擁有外在美貌是不夠的，即使那會使得美貌的人更貼近他們的夢想。可是，還有其他事情是需要考量的。財富和百萬富翁在想什麼的秘訣將幫助妳更進一步地了解那些百萬富翁們在想些什麼。

B. Although people are reluctant to admit the fact that luck does play a key role in determining how one gets picked by a millionaire, luck is surely more important than other factors, such as diploma and appearances. In *Match Point*, Nola is an overly attractive knockout, but Tom's mother has obviously not been a big fan of her, which makes her way to the marriage faltering and stagnated. During the conversation with his friend Chris, Tom confides that "It's taken mother a while to get used to the idea that I'm serious about her. Mother's always had this funny little agenda for me which doesn't involve marrying a struggling actress." At a much later time, Nola is constantly being questioned by Tom's mother Eleanor. The innuendos include "It's a particular cruel business for a woman and as you get older and time passes if nothing happens it gets harder and harder. But I am a great one for facing up to realities." Of course, the chat goes unpleasant for both parties as Tom raises the voice to his mother. Chris, on the other hand, has been getting the preference for Tom's parents that leads to a completely different outcome. Chris even gets married with Tom's sister.

儘管人們不願承認，幸運確實在如何被百萬富翁挑選到扮演著關鍵的角色，幸運確實是比起其他像是文憑和外貌的因素更為重要。在《愛情決勝點》，諾拉是位極具吸引力的美人，但是湯姆的母親顯然不太喜愛她，這樣讓她的婚姻之路走的搖搖欲墜和停滯不前。在與他的朋友克里斯的談話中，湯姆吐露「耗費一大段時間，母親才逐漸習慣著我對諾拉的感情是認真看待的。母親對我總是有些有趣的安排，但這並不包含跟一個難以謀生的女演員結婚」。在更之後，諾拉不斷地受到湯姆的母親旖蓮娜的質問。諷刺的話語包含了「演藝事業對女人來説是個特別殘酷的事業，而隨著時間流逝，妳容貌不在，如果還是不成的話，只會越來越艱辛。但像我來説，我就很勇於面對現實面」。當然，這樣的談話對雙方來説都不悦耳，隨著湯姆跟母親的講話聲音越來越大。克里斯，卻相反地，受到湯姆父母的偏好，而有全然不同的結果。克里斯甚至跟湯姆的妹妹結為連理。

C. The luck theory of getting liked by the millionaire's parents can be further proved by several storylines in *Desperate Housewives*. After the ending of the first marriage, Gaby is pursued by Victor, who is extremely wealthy. Gaby seems to know every Victor's move and outmaneuvers him on the surface, but what she has failed to notice is that Victor is using her to get more votes for certain groups. She learns the news on her wedding day by inadvertently overhearing the conversation between Victor and his father. Beforehand, his father skillfully saves the couple's quarreling over something trivial. Then again in a later time, when Gaby leaves a telephone message, saying that she is leaving him. Victor's father once again beguiles Gaby by saying she can freely add zeros on the check, if she leaves Victor after the election. The manipulation works. It is not until Victor's funeral does Gaby realize that the money is all in Victor's father name, and Victor has no money. Gaby cannot clinch her father-in-law.

受到百萬富翁的父母喜歡的幸運理論也能夠在慾望師奶的故事主線中得到證實。在第一次的婚姻結束時,蓋比受到維克特的追求,而維克特相當有錢。在表面上,蓋比甚至知道維克特的每個追求舉動並且都智勝維克特,但是她未能察覺到的是維克特是為了要利用她獲取特定族群的票源。最終,她在婚禮上不經意地得知這件事情,她偷聽到維克特和他父親的談話。早先,維克特的父親還巧妙地化解了小倆口對於瑣事的紛爭。接著在更之後,當蓋比留下電話訊息,告知她決定要離開維克特。維克特的父親再一次地蒙騙蓋比説,她可以在支票上隨意地加上很多零,如果她選擇在選舉後才離開維克特。這樣的操作又奏效了。直到最後維克特葬禮時,蓋比才意識到錢一直都在維克特父親名下,維克特壓根沒有錢。蓋比始終無法勝過她的公公。

D. In *Desperate Housewives*, luck does work in Susan's favor when she starts the relationship with the multi-millionaire, Ian. Ian is incredibly rich with a castle, but like what's in Gaby's case and Nola's situation, the groom's parents are the key to a successful marriage. The marriage cannot even have a start if there is a veto from Ian's parents. The meeting with Ian's parents goes well until Susan makes a comment that raises a red flag for Ian's mother. Later, Ian's mother has a serious talk with them both, saying that if she eventually gets a divorce with Ian, she will accept a cash settlement and not go after the property and the castile Ian inherits from them. Even though Susan comes up with other way to avoid signing the pre-nuptial agreement, her relationship with Ian does not work out.

在《慾望師奶》，幸運確實站在蘇珊那頭，當她開始了跟怡安談戀愛。怡安非常有錢且有個城堡，但是就如同蓋比的案例和諾拉的情況，新郎的父母是婚姻成功的關鍵。婚姻甚至無法展開，如果怡安的父母投下了反對票。蘇珊跟怡安的父母的會面進行得很順利，直到蘇珊說了一些話讓怡安的母親舉起了紅旗。之後，怡安的母親與兩人有著嚴肅的談話，說道如果蘇珊最終跟怡安離婚的話，那麼她要接受金錢的解決方案，而不能提出要求索取怡安將從兩老手中繼承的地產和城堡。即使蘇珊想出了其他的辦法免掉簽署婚前協議，她跟怡安的感情關係最終也沒有結果。

E. Aside from getting liked by the parents of the millionaire, what most people don't know is the fact that rich people are unwilling to give the company's stock to their spouse. This can be verified in both

Revenge and *Grinding it out*. In *Revenge*, Victoria is smart and competent, but during the divorce, her ex-husband makes an excuse of saying he doesn't want to let his father down. He can only give Victoria the house, the deed of the Grayson Manor, even if Victoria asks him about the shares of the company. *Grinding it out* shares a similar vein. Ray doesn't want to give the shares of McDonald to his first wife because that's too valuable. He is only willing to give his first wife something tangible, such as the house.

除了受到百萬富翁的父母的喜歡之外，大多數人所不知道的是，有錢人不願意將公司的股份給予自己的另一半。這點能夠分別在《復仇》和《永不放棄我如何打造麥當勞王國》中得到證實。在《復仇》，維多利亞聰明且有能力，但在離婚時，她前夫編了一個謊言說，他不想要讓自己父親失望。他僅願意給維多利亞房子，也就是葛雷森莊園的產權，即使維多利亞詢問他關於公司的股份。《永不放棄我如何打造麥當勞王國》也與之雷同。雷不想要給他首任妻子麥當勞的股份，因為該股份價值連城。他僅願意給他首任妻子實體的東西，例如房子。

READING PASSAGE 2

You should spend about 20 minutes on **Questions 14-27**
which are based on Reading Passage 2 below.

A Tale of Two Cities:
Two Major Trials That Help You
Get the Gist Without Reading the Book

A. Two major trials in A Tale of Two Cities, and two men who bear a strong resemblance, have intertwined a gripping love story that endures the test of time. One is a treason crime, and the other the crime of being the aristocratic fugitive.

B. Upon the arrival in England, Charles Darnay is hauled into a lawsuit. During the treason crime trial, it is to be decided whether several witnesses' testimonies are strong enough to convict Charles Darnay. Several witnesses are called, including Lucie Manette and Dr. Manette, and lawyers have been arguing intently literally at court. Darnay's acquittal rests on the lawyer's statement that his likeness to Sydney Carton might indicate that the person can be anyone, further weakening British spies' testimony. Eventually he is released.

C. Lucie Manette and Charles Darnay have known each other

You should spend about 20 minutes on **Questions 14-27**, which are based on Reading Passage 2 below.

A Tale of Two Cities:
Two Major Trials That Help You
Get the Gist Without Reading the Book

A. Two major trials in *A Tale of Two Cities*, and two men who bear a strong resemblance have intertwined a gripping love story that endures the test of time. One is a treason crime, and the other the crime of being the aristocratic fugitive.

B. Upon the arrival in England, Charles Darnay is lapsed into a lawsuit. During the treason crime trial, it is to be decided whether several witnesses' testimonies are strong enough to convict Charles Darnay. Several witnesses are called, including Lucie Manette and Dr. Manette, and lawyers have been arguing intermittently at court. Darnay's acquittal rests on the lawyer's statement that his likeness to Sydney Carton might indicate that the person can be anyone, further weakening British spies' testimony. Eventually, he is released.

C. Lucie Manette and Charles Darnay have known each other right before the trial. During Lucie's journey back to London, she has received an attentive care from Charles Darnay. Lucie's father used to be confined in prison for 18 years. The imprisonment results from Dr. Manette's resistance of accepting the bribe (money and the rouleau of gold) from Marquis St. Evremonde. Dr. Manette is first forced to do the diagnosis for Evremonde. Then he witnesses a criminally atrocious act done by Evremonde.

D. Dr. Manette's imprisonment in the Bastille makes him miserably secluded. His wife has had a yearning for him, but two years after Dr. Manette's captivity, she dies. Before she dies, she entrusts the bank to be Lucie's guardian. Thereafter, the infant Lucie is taken by Lorry from Paris to London, and has received the care by kind Miss Pross, the servant. Meanwhile, Dr. Manette is released from the prison, and is making a living by manufacturing shoes, a skill that he learns during his incarceration. Then comes the shocking revelation that Dr. Manette is still alive, so Lucie and Lorry go to the old servant's house. There Lucie finds her father is living in a narrow space, but it serves as a great place for people like his father, who has a long departure from the real world. Lucie seems agitated while seeing him, and Lucie has made a decision of taking her father back to London. This has led to their encounter with Charles Darnay.

E. After the ending of Charles Darnay's trial, Lucie and his father now live in London, where Dr. Manette resumes his doctor business and has an excellent reputation. As Dr. Manette's condition has become better, Lucie is optimistic about her future prospect. Aside from her family life, Lucie's love life also blossoms. Other than Charles Darnay, Sydney Carton and another lawyer Stryver have also shown an interest in her. However, Carton is diagnosed with lung cancer and Stryver is disqualified by Lucie's standards, leaving Charles Darnay the only option for Lucie. Soon Lucie and Charles Darnay get married and have a kid. Simultaneously, Carton never ceases loving Lucie, yet he suppresses the love.

F. While Lucie and Darnay have been living happily thereafter, a revolution is happening in France. With Darnay's parents passing away and Marquis st Evremonde meeting his doom by getting killed by a peasant's father, Madame Defarge has since then woven scarfs that contain vile acts of those aristocrats. Among these messages, Charles Darnay is included, and the happy life of Lucie is soon obliterated by the imminent accusations of the French populace.

G. Then comes the French revolution with aristocrats getting beheaded one after another. During the chaos, Charles Darnay has received Gabelle's letter, stating the fact that he is faced with a death penalty. Of course, Charles Darnay comes to Gabelle's rescue without realizing that he will put himself in danger. He is soon recognized by others, and has led to a second trial upon his arrival in Paris. The trial is breathtaking. Dr. Manette's testimony is the most convincing and is strong enough to get Charles Darnay acquitted. Dr. Manette's prison life in the Bastille is the living proof, but the wicked Madame Defarge has the document that Dr. Manette wrote during his unfair incarceration. That is a downside for the defendant, Charles Darnay during his re-trial because it has provided a probative burden on him. A piece of evidence like that is considered definitive, and it has been adduced as a proof of his guilt. Charles Darnay is; thus, sentenced to death.

H. Lucie and her father's appalling countenances might signal the message that Charles Darnay's fate is doomed, a dire blow for both of them. However, there is another kind of love that you do not necessarily have to be with the person you love, and you are willing to make a sacrifice as long as the person you love will be happy. Sydney Carton's ultimate sacrifice has a rich connotation, changing the inexorable fate of Darnay. In the end, Sydney Carton surreptitiously makes an exchange with Charles Darnay in the cell, changes the cloth and waits for the death penalty...

Questions 14-19

Complete each sentence with the correct ending, A-J below.

Write the correct letter, A-J, in boxes 14-19 on your answer sheet.

14 During the treason trial, Charles Darnay's exoneration is dependent on

15 Dr. Manette's incarceration is due to

16 Charles Darnay's recognition by others has resulted in

17 Dr. Manette's discharge from the prison is considered

18 Charles Darnay and Lucie's expunction in happiness is related to

19 Dr. Manette's stay in prison earns him

A the unanticipated occurrence

B the unbearable seclusion

C the skill of manufacturing shoes

D the unwillingness of accepting the bribe

E the resemblance of his countenance to another lawyer

F the long departure from the real world

G the riot of the English populace

H the death penalty

I the incrimination of the plebs living in the area

J the litigation upon his advent in the country

Questions 20-27

Complete the summary using the list of words and phrases A-Q below

Write the correct letter, A-Q in boxes 20-27 on your answer sheet.

A Tale of Two Cities	EVENTS
Relating to Sydney Carton	• Charles Darnay's **20.**_____ destiny is overturned by Sydney Carton's willingness to make a sacrifice, making the story touching and gripping. • Before Sydney Carton's move in the cell, the sentence has been a **21.**_____ whack for both Dr. Manette and Lucie. • Sydney Carton even has an **22.**_____ that prevents him from pursuing Lucie.

The second trial	• Before the trial, Madame Defarge has been seen weaving scarfs that are made up of **23.**_____ acts of those aristocrats. Among these messages, Charles Darnay is included
	• Among them, Dr. Manette's statement will be most **24.**_____ because he was once incarcerated in the Bastille.
	• Madame Defarge possesses the writing of Dr. Manette, and this can be **25.**_____ for the accused.
	• The document is viewed as **26.**_____ during his re-trial.
Relating to Marquis St. Evremonde	• Marquis St. Evremonde is the main reason why Dr. Manette's miserably secluded.
	• Marquis St. Evremonde offers a cylindrical packet of **27.**_____ to buy off Dr. Manette and covers his conduct.

Boxes	
A untrustworthy	**B** conclusive
C cheerful	**D** disadvantageous
E dreadful	**F** believable
G fortunate	**H** gold
I money	**J** undetermined
K illness	**L** inescapable
M misfortune	**N** contemptible
O confidential	**P** beneficial
Q seclusion	**R** isolated

11 ｜英國文學＋法律＋歷史

《*A Tale of Two Cities*》

一個動人的偉大愛情故事

　　在答題前第一個步驟是先快速掃視題目題型並快速制定答題策略，在這篇很快可以看到完成句子配對題和摘要式填空，可以一併回答或者是先答摘要式填空。

◆ **第 20 題**，Charles Darnay's **20.**＿＿＿＿＿＿ destiny is overturned by Sydney Carton's willingness to make a sacrifice, making the story touching and gripping⋯，這部分可以對應到 Lucie and her father's appalling countenances might signal the message that Charles Darnay's **fate is doomed**, a dire blow for both of them.，故答案要選 **L** inescapable。is **doomed** 等同於 **inescapable**。

◆ **第 21 題**，Before Sydney Carton's move in the cell, the sentence has been a **21.**＿＿＿＿＿＿ whack for both Dr. Manette and Lucie.，這部分可以對應到 Lucie and her father's appalling countenances might signal the message that Charles Darnay's fate is doomed, **a dire blow** for both of them.，**blow** 等同於 **whack**，故答案要選 **E** dreadful。

- 第 **22** 題，Sydney Carton even has an **22.**＿＿＿＿＿ that prevents him from pursuing Lucie.，這部分可以對應到 However, Carton is diagnosed with lung cancer and Stryver is disqualified by Lucie's standards, leaving Charles Darnay the only option for Lucie.，故答案要選 **K** illness。**lung cancer** 等同於 **illness**。

- 第 **23** 題，. Before the trial, Madame Defarge has been seen weaving scarfs that comprising **23.**＿＿＿＿＿ acts of those aristocrats. Among these messages, Charles Darnay is included，這部分可以對應到 With Darnay's parents passing away and Marquis st Evremonde meeting his doom by getting killed by a peasant's father, Madame Defarge has since then woven scarfs that contain vile acts of those aristocrats.，故答案要選 **N** contemptible。**vile** 等同於 **contemptible**。

- 第 **24** 題，. Among them, Dr. Manette's statement will be most **24.**＿＿＿＿＿ because he was once incarcerated in the Bastille.，這部分可以對應到 Dr. Manette's testimony is the most convincing and is strong enough to get Charles Darnay acquitted.，故答案要選 **F** believable。**convincing** 等同於 **believable**。

- 第 **25** 題，Madame Defarge possesses the writing of Dr. Manette, and this can be **25.** _____ for the accused..，這部分可以對應到 Dr. Manette's prison life in the Bastille is the living proof, but the wicked Madame Defarge has the document that Dr. Manette wrote during his unfair incarceration. That is a downside for the defendant, Charles Darnay during his re-trial because it provides a probative burden on him.，故**答案要選 D** disadvantageous。**disadvantageous** 等同於 **downside**。

- 第 **26** 題，The document is viewed as **26.** _____ during his re-trial.，這部分可以對應到 That is a downside for the defendant, Charles Darnay during his re-trial because it provides a probative burden on him. A piece of evidence like that is considered definitive, and it has been adduced as a proof of his guilt.，故**答案要選 B** conclusive。**definitive** 等同於 **conclusive**。

- 第 **27** 題，Marquis St. Evremonde offers a cylindrical packet of **27.** _____ to buy off Dr. Manette and covers his conduct.，這部分可以對應到 The imprisonment results from Dr. Manette's resistance of accepting the bribe (money and the rouleau of gold) from Marquis St. Evremonde.，故**答案要選 H** gold。括弧內的訊息通常都是考點。**rouleau** 等同於 **a cylindrical packet**。

◆ 第 **14** 題，**14** During the treason trial, Charles Darnay's exoneration is dependent on.，這部分可以對應到 Several witnesses are called, including Lucie Manette and Dr. Manette, and lawyers have been arguing intermittently at court. Darnay's acquittal rests on the lawyer's statement that his likeness to Sydney Carton might indicate that the person can be anyone, further weakening British spies' testimony. Eventually, he is released.，故答案要選 **E** the resemblance of his countenance to another lawyer。

◆ 第 **15** 題，**15** Dr. Manette's incarceration is due to，這部分可以對應到 The imprisonment results from Dr. Manette's resistance of accepting the bribe (money and the rouleau of gold) from Marquis St. Evremonde.，故答案要選 **D** the unwillingness of accepting the bribe。

◆ 第 **16** 題，**16** Charles Darnay's recognition by others has resulted in，這部分可以對應到 Of course, Charles Darnay comes to Gabelle's rescue without realizing that he will put himself in danger. He is soon recognized by others, and has led to a second trial upon his arrival in Paris.，故答案要選 **J** the litigation upon his advent in the country。

- 第 **17** 題，**17** Dr. Manette's discharge from the prison is considered.，這部分可以對應到 Meanwhile, Dr. Manette is released from the prison, and is making a living by manufacturing shoes, a skill that he learns during his incarceration. Then comes the shocking revelation that Dr. Manette is still alive, so Lucie and Lorry go to the old servant's house.，故**答案要選 A** the unanticipated occurrence。

- 第 **18** 題，**18** Charles Darnay and Lucie's expunction in happiness is related to，這部分可以對應到. Among these messages, Charles Darnay is included, and the happiness life of Lucie is soon obliterated by the imminent accusations of the French populace.，故**答案要選 I** the incrimination of the plebs living in the area。

- 第 **19** 題，**19** Dr. Manette's stay in prison earns him，這部分可以對應到 Meanwhile, Dr. Manette is released from the prison, and is making a living by manufacturing shoes, a skill that he learns during his incarceration.，故**答案要選 C** the skill of manufacturing shoes。

聽讀整合 TEST 4 P2

Two major trials in *A Tale of Two Cities*, and two men who bear a strong **1.**_____ have intertwined a gripping love story that endures the test of time. One is a **2.**_____ crime, and the other the crime of being the aristocratic **3.**_____. Upon the arrival in England, Charles Darnay is lapsed into a **4.**_____. During the treason crime trial, it is to be decided whether several witnesses' **5.**_____ are strong enough to convict Charles Darnay. Several witnesses are called, including Lucie Manette and Dr. Manette, and lawyers have been arguing **6.**_____ at court. Darnay's **7.**_____ rests on the lawyer's statement that his **8.**_____ to Sydney Carton might indicate that the person can be anyone, further weakening British spies' testimony. Eventually, he is released.

Lucie Manette and Charles Darnay have known each other right before the trial. During Lucie's journey back to London, she has received an attentive care from Charles Darnay. Lucie's father used to be **9.**_____ in prison for 18 years. The **10.**_____ results from Dr. Manette's resistance of accepting the bribe (money and the **11.**_____ of gold) from Marquis St. Evremonde. Dr. Manette is first forced to do the **12.**_____ for Evremonde. Then he witnesses a criminally **13.**_____ act done by Evremonde.

Dr. Manette's imprisonment in the Bastille makes him miserably **14.**_____. His wife has had a yearning for him, but two years after Dr. Manette's **15.**_____, she dies. Before she dies, she entrusts the bank to be Lucie's guardian. Thereafter, the infant Lucie is taken by Lorry from **16.**_____ to London, and has received the care by kind Miss Pross, the servant. Meanwhile, Dr. Manette is released from the prison, and is making a living by manufacturing shoes, a skill that he learns during his **17.**_____. Then comes the shocking revelation that Dr. Manette is still alive, so Lucie and Lorry go to the old servant's house....Lucie seems **18.**_____ while seeing him, and Lucie has made a decision of taking her father back to London. This has led to their encounter with Charles Darnay.

After the ending of Charles Darnay's trial, Lucie and his father now live in London, where Dr. Manette resumes his **19.**_____ ____ business and has an excellent reputation. As Dr. Manette's condition has become better, Lucie is optimistic about her future **20.**_____. Aside from her family life, Lucie's love life also blossoms. Other than Charles Darnay, Sydney Carton and another lawyer Stryver have also shown an interest in her. However, Carton is diagnosed with lung cancer and Stryver is disqualified by Lucie's standards, leaving Charles Darnay the only option for Lucie. Soon Lucie and Charles Darnay get married and have a kid. Simultaneously, Carton never ceases loving Lucie, yet he **21.**____ _____ the love. While Lucie and Darnay have been living happily thereafter, a revolution is happening in France. With Darnay's parents passing away and Marquis st Evremonde meeting his doom by getting killed by a peasant's father, Madame Defarge has since then woven **22.**_____ that contain **23.**_____ acts of those **24.**_____. Among these messages, Charles Darnay is included, and the happy life of

Lucie is soon obliterated by the **25.**_____ accusations of the French populace.

Then comes the French revolution with aristocrats getting **26.**_____ one after another. During the chaos, Charles Darnay has received Gabelle's letter, stating the fact that he is faced with a death **27.**_____. Of course, Charles Darnay comes to Gabelle's rescue without realizing that he will put himself in danger. He is soon **28.**_____ by others, and has led to a second trial upon his arrival in Paris. The trial is breathtaking. Dr. Manette's testimony is the most convincing and is strong enough to get Charles Darnay acquitted. Dr. Manette's prison life in the Bastille is the living proof, but the wicked Madame Defarge has the **29.**_____ that Dr. Manette wrote during his unfair incarceration. That is a downside for the **30.**_____, Charles Darnay during his re-trial because it has provided a **31.**_____ burden on him. A piece of evidence like that is considered **32.**_____, and it has been **33.**_____ as a proof of his guilt. Charles Darnay is; thus, sentenced to death.

Lucie and her father's appalling **34.**_____ might signal the message that Charles Darnay's fate is doomed, a **35.**_____ blow for both of them. However, there is another kind of love that you do not necessarily have to be with the person you love, and you are willing to make a sacrifice as long as the person you love will be happy. Sydney Carton's ultimate sacrifice has a rich connotation, changing the **36.**_____ fate of Darnay....

A. Two major trials in *A Tale of Two Cities*, and two men who bear a strong resemblance have intertwined a gripping love story that endures the test of time. One is a treason crime, and the other the crime of being the aristocratic fugitive.

在《雙城記》中的兩場主要的審判和兩位長得相似的兩個男子交織出一個扣人心弦、經得起時間檢驗的愛情故事。其中一個是叛國罪，而另一個則是身為貴族的逃犯。

B. Upon the arrival in England, Charles Darnay is lapsed into a lawsuit. During the treason crime trial, it is to be decided whether several witnesses' testimonies are strong enough to convict Charles Darnay. Several witnesses are called, including Lucie Manette and Dr. Manette, and lawyers have been arguing intermittently at court. Darnay's acquittal rests on the lawyer's statement that his likeness to Sydney Carton might indicate that the person can be anyone, further weakening British spies' testimony. Eventually, he is released.

在抵達英國後，查爾斯·達內就捲入了一場官司。在叛國罪的審判期間，幾位證人的證詞是否有力以將查爾斯·達內定

Test 4

TEST 1
TEST 2
TEST 3
TEST 4

Reading Passage 2

罪，會將做出裁決。幾位證人受到傳喚，當中包含了露西・曼奈特和曼奈特醫生，而律師們一直不斷地在庭上爭論著。達內的無罪開釋仰賴著律師的證詞，他和雪梨・卡頓的長相相似可能顯示出那個人可以是任何人，進一步地弱化了英國間諜們的證詞。最終，他獲釋。

C. Lucie Manette and Charles Darnay have known each other right before the trial. During Lucie's journey back to London, she has received an attentive care from Charles Darnay. Lucie's father used to be confined in prison for 18 years. The imprisonment results from Dr. Manette's resistance of accepting the bribe (money and the rouleau of gold) from Marquis St. Evremonde. Dr. Manette is first forced to do the diagnosis for Evremonde. Then he witnesses a criminally atrocious act done by Evremonde.

早在審判前，露西・曼奈特和查爾斯・達內就已經認識彼此。在露西回到倫敦的旅途中，她受到查爾斯・達內的妥善照顧。露西的父親過去曾在監獄中被關 18 年。牢獄之災導因於曼奈特醫生拒絕接受厄弗裡蒙地侯爵的賄賂（金錢和用紙包附的一捲黃金）。曼奈特醫生先是被迫替厄弗裡蒙地侯爵看診。緊接著，他目睹了厄弗裡蒙地侯爵殘暴的罪行。

D. Dr. Manette's imprisonment in the Bastille makes him miserably secluded. His wife has had a yearning for him, but two years after Dr. Manette's captivity, she dies. Before she dies, she entrusts the bank to be Lucie's guardian. Thereafter, the infant Lucie is taken by Lorry from Paris to London, and has received the care by kind Miss Pross, the servant. Meanwhile, Dr. Manette is released from the prison, and is making a living by manufacturing shoes, a skill that he learns during his incarceration. Then comes the shocking revelation that Dr. Manette is still alive, so Lucie and Lorry go to the old servant's house. There Lucie finds her father is living in a narrow space, but it serves as a great place for people like his father, who has a long departure from the real world. Lucie seems agitated while seeing him, and Lucie has made a decision of taking her father back to London. This has led to their encounter with Charles Darnay.

曼奈特醫生在巴士底獄的牢獄之災使他悲慘地與世隔絕。他的妻子對他有著思念，但在曼奈特醫生坐牢的兩年後，她與世長辭了。在她死之前，她委託銀行當露西的監護人。爾後，還是嬰孩的露西就被羅里從巴黎帶到了倫敦，並且受到善良的僕人，波西小姐照顧。與此同時，曼奈特醫生從監獄中獲釋並且以製鞋為生，一項他從坐牢中所學到的技能。接著一個意想不到的驚人真相揭露了，曼奈特醫生仍在世上，所以露西和羅里前往舊僕人的房子。在那裡，露西發現她的父親生活在狹窄的空間裡，但這個地方卻對像是他父親這樣的人來説是適得其所，因為他父親跟真實世界有很大的脱節。在看到她父親時，露西激動異常，而她做了將父親帶回倫敦的決定。這也促成了她們和查爾斯‧達內的偶遇。

E. After the ending of Charles Darnay's trial, Lucie and his father now live in London, where Dr. Manette resumes his doctor business and has an excellent reputation. As Dr. Manette's condition has become better, Lucie is optimistic about her future prospect. Aside from her family life, Lucie's love life also blossoms. Other than Charles Darnay, Sydney Carton and another lawyer Stryver have also shown an interest in her. However, Carton is diagnosed with lung cancer and Stryver is disqualified by Lucie's standards, leaving Charles Darnay the only option for Lucie. Soon Lucie and Charles Darnay get married and have a kid. Simultaneously, Carton never ceases loving Lucie, yet he suppresses the love.

在查爾斯‧達內的審判結束後，露西和她的父親現在生活在倫敦，而曼奈特醫生接續從事他醫生的事業且享譽盛名。隨著曼奈特醫生的狀況漸入佳境，露西對於自己的未來感到樂觀。除了她的家庭生活之外，露西的愛情生活也生氣蓬勃。除了查爾斯‧達內之外，雪梨‧卡頓和另一名律師史特佛爾都對露西感興趣。然而，卡頓因診斷出肺炎，而史特佛爾並未達到露西的標準，讓查爾斯・達內成了露西的唯一選擇。很快地，露西和查爾斯・達內結為連理並有一名小孩。同時，卡頓並未停止對露西的愛，但他卻選擇壓抑住愛情。

F. While Lucie and Darnay have been living happily thereafter, a revolution is happening in France. With Darnay's parents passing away and Marquis st Evremonde meeting his doom by getting killed by a peasant's father, Madame Defarge has since then woven scarfs that contain vile acts of those aristocrats. Among these messages, Charles Darnay is included, and the happy life of Lucie is soon obliterated by the imminent accusations of the French populace.

當露西和達內就此過著幸福快樂的日子的同時，在法國一場革命就此展開了。隨著達內的父母相繼過世，以及厄弗裡蒙地侯爵受到報應被農人的父親殺死，德法奇夫人從那個時候就開始將含有那些貴族的惡行編織在圍巾上頭。在那些訊息中，查爾斯・達內就包含在內，而露西的快樂生活也馬上因為即將到來的法國民眾的控訴而化為烏有。

G. Then comes the French revolution with aristocrats getting beheaded one after another. During the chaos, Charles Darnay has received Gabelle's letter, stating the fact that he is faced with a death penalty. Of course, Charles Darnay comes to Gabelle's rescue without realizing that he will put himself in danger. He is soon recognized by others, and has led to a second trial upon his arrival in Paris. The trial is breathtaking. Dr. Manette's testimony is the most convincing and is strong enough to get Charles Darnay acquitted. Dr. Manette's prison life in the Bastille is the living proof, but the wicked Madame Defarge has the document that Dr. Manette wrote during his unfair incarceration. That is a downside for the defendant, Charles Darnay during his re-trial because it has provided a probative burden on him. A piece of evidence like that is considered definitive, and it has been adduced as a proof of his guilt. Charles Darnay is; thus, sentenced to death.

接著就是法國革命，隨著貴族們一個接著一個的受到斬首。在混亂之中，查爾斯·達內收到了蓋博爾的信，信中陳述著自己面臨死刑的判決。當然，查爾斯·達內前往拯救蓋博爾，卻並未意識到自己猶如羊入虎口。達內也馬上被其他人認了出來，並促成了在他抵達法國的時候的第二場審判。審判過程令人屏息。曼奈特醫生的證詞是最具有說服力的，強而有力到足以能讓查爾斯·達內脫罪。曼奈特醫生在巴士底獄的監獄生活就是栩栩如生的證據，但是邪惡的德法奇夫人握有曼奈特醫生在他自己處於不公的牢獄之災時所撰寫的文件。這對被告查爾斯‧達內的重審來説是不利的，因為文件將供作證據而對他形成負擔。像那樣的證據會被視為是具有決定性的，而且將會因此而引證為他有罪的證據。查爾斯‧達內因此被判處了死刑。

H. Lucie and her father's appalling countenances might signal the message that Charles Darnay's fate is doomed, a dire blow for both of them. However, there is another kind of love that you do not necessarily have to be with the person you love, and you are willing to make a sacrifice as long as the person you love will be happy. Sydney Carton's ultimate sacrifice has a rich connotation, changing the inexorable fate of Darnay. In the end, Sydney Carton surreptitiously makes an exchange with Charles Darnay in the cell, changes the cloth and waits for the death penalty...

露西和她父親的觸目心驚的面容可能暗示了訊息，就是查爾斯‧達內命數已定，這對他們兩人來説是個悲慘的打擊。然而，世間上有另一種愛情是，你不一定要跟你所愛的人在一起，而是你願意做出犧牲，只要那個你所愛的人過得快樂。雪梨‧卡頓的最終犧牲有著豐富的意涵，改變了達內無法逆轉的命運。最後，在獄中，雪梨‧卡頓暗中將自己和查爾斯‧達內做出替換、換上衣物，然後等待死刑的到來…。

You should spend about 20 minutes on **Questions 28-40**
which are based on Reading Passage 3 below

Sociology and Psychology Study:
Why the Success Cannot Endure

A. Contrast to what we might have expected from the fashion assistant who has to be the stereotype by being stunningly beautiful, Betty Suarez is unique in her own way. That makes her get picked by Bradford Meade, the owner of the Meade Publications, her coworker Marc St James is also a peculiar assistant, and the two might have been the best pick for their role as assistant. It goes to show that in addition to appearance, experience, and fashion sense, personal qualities are the key to get to the top or get the job done. Each possesses uniquely quirky traits that make them a suitable and loyal candidate for both their bosses, Slater and Daniel.

B. One of the daunting tasks given to Betty to see if she truly has what it takes to be Slater's successor is getting the crown. It was also the task once given to Slater by her scary boss, Fey Sommer. Getting the crown is not as easy as it sounds, and Slater had to do numerous scheming to get it.

You should spend about 20 minutes on **Questions 28-40**, which are based on Reading Passage 3 below.

Sociology and Psychology Study: Why the Success Cannot Endure

A. Contrast to what we might have expected from the fashion assistant who has to be the stereotype by being stunningly beautiful, Betty Suarez is unique in her own way. That makes her get picked by Bradford Meade, the owner of the Meade Publications. Her coworker Marc St James is also a peculiar assistant, and the two might have been the best pick for their role as assistants. It goes to show that in addition to appearance, experience, and fashion sense, personal qualities are the key to get to the top or get the job down. Each possesses uniquely quirky traits that make them a suitable and loyal candidate for both their bosses, Slater and Daniel.

B. One of the daunting tasks given to Betty to see if she truly has what it takes to be Slater's successor is getting the crown. It was also the task once given to Slater by her scary boss, Fey Sommer. Getting the crown is not as easy as it sounds, and Slater had to use numerous scheming to get it.

C. This happens right after Betty has helped Slater land a major advertiser during the meeting. Slater has listed multiple things for Betty to accomplish, and one of them is the tiara that Catherine the Great wore at her wedding to Peter III. Betty views this as a punishment for her conduct at the meeting, but in fact it is a test to see if she is qualified for the job. She successfully accomplishes all tasks, including lending the tiara, and that makes her outshine another assistant Marc.

D. Marc jokes about her way of getting the tiara by listening to the curator's whining and crying. By being nice to someone is the key to lend the tiara. One does not necessarily have to do the nasty things to get the job done. The deal for getting the tiara also includes a full-page ad in the next month's issue. An ad space in exchange for using the tiara for 48 hours. Slater later says that "my methods were a little less wholesome than yours." and "there's been only one other person who's been able to get that tiara." Accomplishing a seemingly impossible task has proved that Betty has rare potential. One cannot argue that it's not her quirkiness.

E. Another incident relating to Betty's uniqueness is the tico berry shoot. Kimmie sabotages the shoot by saying "have fun doing a tico berry shoot with no tico berries." Then she throws all the berries into a large pond, leaving all people stunned. With Betty's two bosses, Slater and Daniel staring at her, Betty tries to think outside the box, and she is the one who saves the day.

F. From Betty's life at Mode, how one person can be successful can be illuminated. In *America's Next Top Model*, during the deliberation of a particular episode, Tyra Bank, the host of the show, was asked about the same question as to how success of most winners of the show cannot last, and it was even before the publication of the bestseller, *Quirky*. There must be something, she explained, such as quirkiness, that makes them special.

G. The answer is quite meaningful and insightful, and we must not forget the fact that all judges have their preferences that create a bias against those who are truly great. Sometimes those judges have to pick the person who suits the image for the cover girl and the magazine that they have been working with in that particular season.

H. For those who have participated the reality show, you simply cannot take the winning too seriously. It is great that if you eventually win the prize, but if you don't win and keep doing what you love and you will eventually find another way. You probably do not win, but that doesn't mean that you are not great. It probably conveys the message that your picture and style do not suit the company's ideal. There are other companies that are a great match for you. Not to mention, you have the exposure from attending the show, and multiple people who are currently working in that industry get to see something from you by watching the show.

I. This further explains the fact that why some candidates who do not win but eventually are more successful than those who do. Let's not forget that ultimately it is those fans who purchase the record, magazine or advertised products not those judges. Perhaps you have that quirkiness in you that you do not know it yet. That does not have to be physically attractive. Follow your heart and eventually will embark on a journey that amazes people around you.

Questions 28-34

Reading Passage 3 has nine paragraphs, A-I

Choose the correct heading for each paragraph from the list of headings below.

Write the correct number, i-xii, in boxes 28-34 on your answer sheet.

List of Headings

i the credit of getting the major advertiser

ii formidable assignment given by a higher up

iii using wholesome methods is the key

iv difficulty of gathering tico berries

v peculiarity is the key to accomplish the task

vi distinctive idiosyncrasy is the explanation

vii acumen that answers the puzzle

viii one's greatness cannot be determined by the judges

ix an examine that can measure one's capability

x quirkiness proves to be helpful in another case

xi the importance of the publication

xii prejudices are inevitable

---

28 Paragraph A

29 Paragraph B

30 Paragraph C

31 Paragraph D

32 Paragraph E

33 Paragraph F

34 Paragraph G

Questions 35-40

Complete the summary below

Choose No More Than One Word from the passage for each answer

Write your answers in boxes 35-38 on your answer sheet.

Both Fey Sommer and Slater have used the task of getting the tiara to choose their **35.**_____. Unlike Slater, who utilized lots of scheming to accomplish the task, Betty takes **36.**_____ feelings by heart to get the crown. Betty's approaches are **37.**_____ wholesome than those of the Slater. The tiara is not free, and the deal is comprised of a full-page ad in exchange for using the tiara for **38.**_____ days. Accomplishing a seemingly impossible task has proved that Betty has rare potential.

In the reality show, you do not have to take winning too seriously. Even if you do not win, you have already gotten the **39.**_____. There might be some audiences that recognize your potential by watching the show. Eventually, your future will not be determined by those **40.**_____, and you will find another way to get there.

解析

12 ｜商管＋心理學＋社會學

《*Ugly Betty*》、《*Quirky*》和《全美超模》
探究為什麼實境秀選出來的冠、亞軍，在賽後卻無法長紅

　　在答題前第一個步驟是先快速掃視題目題型並快速制定答題策略，在這篇很快可以看到段落標題試題和摘要題，可以先寫段落標題邊順讀答題，最後攻略摘要題。

◆ **第 28 題**，**28 Paragraph A**，主要可以對應到 Contrast to what we might expect from the fashion assistant who has to be the stereotype by being stunningly beautiful, Betty Suarez is unique in her own way. That makes her get picked by Bradford Meade, the owner of the Meade Publications. Her coworker Marc St James is also a peculiar assistant, and the two might have been the best pick for their role as assistants. It goes to show that in addition to appearance, experience, and fashion sense, personal qualities are the key to get to the top or get the job down. ，表示不一定要刻板印象中那樣，具備獨特特質就能勝任，**答案要選 vi distinctive idiosyncrasy is the explanation**。

◆ **第 29 題**，**29 Paragraph B**，主要可以對應到 One of the daunting tasks given to Betty to see if she truly has what it takes to be Slater's successor is getting the crown. It was also the task once given to Slater by her scary boss, Fey Sommer. Getting the crown is not as easy as it sounds, and Slater had to use numerous scheming to get it. ，過去 Slater 的主管給過她這項任務，而現在 Betty 亦是，**答案要選 ii formidable assignment given by a higher up**，高層所交付的任務。

♦ **第 30 題**，**30 Paragraph C**，主要可以對應到 Betty views this as a punishment for her conduct at the meeting, but in fact it is a test to see if she is qualified for the job. She successfully accomplishes all tasks, including lending the tiara, and that make her outshine another assistant Marc…. Accomplishing a seemingly impossible task has proved that Betty has rare potential. One cannot argue that it's not her quirkiness. ，主旨其實就是以任務挑選出符合能力者，**答案要選 ix an examine that can measure one's capability**。

♦ **第 31 題**，**31 Paragraph D**，主要可以對應到 Another incident relating to Betty's uniqueness is the tico berry shoot. Kimmie sabotages the shoot by saying "have fun doing a tico berry shoot with no tico berries." Then she throws all the berries into a large pond, leaving all people stunned. With Betty's two bosses, Slater and Daniel staring at her, Betty tries to think outside the box, and she is the one who saves the day，兩項任務都能證明出 Betty 是具有獨特的特質才能完成任務且解決問題，答案要選 **v peculiarity is the key to accomplish the task**。

◆ 第 32 題，**32 Paragraph E**，主要可以對應到 from Betty's life at Mode, how one person can be successful can be illuminated. In America's Top Model, during the deliberation of a particular episode, Tyra Bank, the host of the show, was asked about the same question as to how success of most winners of the show cannot last, and it was even before the publication of the bestseller, *Quirky*. There must be something, she explained, such as quirkiness, that makes them special，答案要選 **x quirkiness proves to be helpful in another case**。

◆ 第 33 題，**33 Paragraph F**，主要可以對應到 the answer is quite meaningful and insightful, and we must not forget the fact that all judges have their preferences that create a bias against those who are truly great. Sometimes those judges have to pick the person who suits the image for the cover girl and the magazine that they work with in that particular season，代表其實這些評估都是有偏見存在其中的，這似乎是無可避免，答案要選 **xii prejudices are inevitable**。

◆ **第 34 題，34 Paragraph G**，主要可以對應到 for those who have participated the reality show, you simply cannot take the winning too seriously. It is great that if you eventually win the prize, but if you don't win and keep doing what you love and you will eventually find another way. You probably do not win, but that doesn't mean that you are not great. It probably conveys the message that your picture and style do not suit the company's ideal. ，一個人的價值和能力並不會因為一個節目就決定了一切，**答案要選 viii one's greatness cannot be determined by the judges**。

◆ **第 35 題**，Both Fey Sommer and Slater have used the task of getting the tiara to choose their **35._____**.可以對應到 one of the daunting tasks given to Betty to see if she truly has what it takes to be Slater's successor is getting the crown. ，故答案要選 **successor**。

◆ **第 36 題**，Unlike Slater, who utilized lots of scheming to accomplish the task, Betty takes **36._____** feelings by heart to get the crown.可以對應到 Marc jokes about her way of getting the tiara by listening to the curator's whining and crying. ，故答案要選 **curator**。

◆ **第 37 題**，Betty's approaches are **37._____**

wholesome than those of the Slater.可以對應到 Slater later says that "my methods were a little less wholesome than yours.",但主詞有調換位置了,故 less 要改成 more,故答案要選 **more**。

♦ 第 **38** 題,The tiara is not free, and the deal is comprised of a full-page ad in exchange for using the tiara for **38.**_____ days. Accomplishing a seemingly impossible task has proved that Betty has rare potential.可以對應到 The deal for getting the tiara also includes a full-page ad in the next month's issue. An ad space in exchange for using the tiara for 48 hours.,要將小時換成天,故 48 小時等同於兩天,故答案要選 **two**。

♦ 第 **39** 題,In the reality show, you do not have to take winning too seriously. Even if you do not win, you have already gotten the **39.**_____.可以對應到 You probably do not win, but that doesn't mean that you are not great. It probably conveys the message that your picture and style do not suit the company's ideal. There are other companies that are a great match for you. Not to mention, you have the **exposure** from attending the show,故答案要選 **exposure**。

◆ **第 40 題**，There might be some audiences that recognize your potential by watching the show. Eventually, your future will not be determined by those **40.** _____, and you will find another way to get there. 可以對應到 Let's not forget that ultimately it is those fans who purchase the record, magazine or advertised products not those judges. ，故答案要選 **judges**。

◆ 全部答完也可以檢視剩下的其他選項，其他選項均為 supporting details。答段落標題題很重要的一點就是區分是主要訊息和細節性訊息。（**i** the credit of getting the major advertiser, **iii** using wholesome methods is the key, **iv** difficulty of gathering tico berries, **vii** acumen that answers the puzzle, **xi** the importance of the publication）

聽讀整合 **TEST 4 P3**

Contrast to what we might have expected from the **1.**_____ assistant who has to be the **2.**_____ by being stunningly beautiful, Betty Suarez is unique in her own way. That makes her get picked by Bradford Meade, the owner of the Meade Publications. Her **3.**_____ Marc St James is also a **4.**_____ assistant, and the two might have been the best pick for their role as assistants. It goes to show that in addition to appearance, experience, and fashion sense, personal **5.**_____ are the key to get to the top or get the job down. Each possesses uniquely **6.**_____ traits that make them a suitable and loyal **7.**_____ for both their bosses, Slater and Daniel.

One of the **8.**_____ tasks given to Betty to see if she truly has what it takes to be Slater's **9.**_____ is getting the crown. It was also the task once given to Slater by her scary boss, Fey Sommer. Getting the crown is not as easy as it sounds, and Slater had to use numerous **10.**_____ to get it. This happens right after Betty has helped Slater land a major **11.**_____ during the meeting. Slater has listed multiple things for Betty to accomplish, and one of them is the tiara that Catherine the Great wore at her wedding to Peter III. Betty views this as a **12.**_____ for her conduct at the meeting, but in fact it is a test to see if she is qualified for the job. She successfully **13.**_____ all tasks, including lending the tiara, and that makes her outshine another assistant Marc.

Marc jokes about her way of getting the tiara by listening to the **14.** _____ whining and crying. By being nice to someone is the key to lend the tiara. One does not necessarily have to do the **15.** _____ things to get the job done. The deal for getting the tiara also includes a full-page ad in the next month's **16.** _____. An ad space in exchange for using the tiara for 48 hours. Slater later says that "my methods were a little less **17.** _____ than yours." and "there's been only one other person who's been able to get that tiara." Accomplishing a seemingly **18.** _____ task has proved that Betty has rare potential. One cannot argue that it's not her quirkiness.

Another incident relating to Betty's uniqueness is the tico berry shoot. Kimmie **19.** _____ the shoot by saying "have fun doing a tico berry shoot with no tico berries." Then she throws all the berries into a large **20.** _____, leaving all people stunned. With Betty's two bosses, Slater and Daniel staring at her, Betty tries to think outside the box, and she is the one who saves the day.

From Betty's life at Mode, how one person can be successful can be **21.** _____. In *America's Next Top Model*, during the **22.** _____ of a particular episode, Tyra Bank, the host of the show, was asked about the same question as to how success of most **23.** _____ of the show cannot last, and it was even before the **24.** _____ of the bestseller, *Quirky*. There must be something, she explained, such as quirkiness, that makes them special. The answer is quite meaningful and **25.** _____, and we must not forget the fact that all judges have their

26._____ that create a bias against those who are truly great. Sometimes those judges have to pick the person who suits the image for the cover girl and the magazine that they have been working with in that particular season.

For those who have participated the **27.**_____ show, you simply cannot take the winning too seriously. It is great that if you eventually win the prize, but if you don't win and keep doing what you love and you will eventually find another way....There are other companies that are a great match for you. Not to mention, you have the **28.**_____ from attending the show, and multiple people who are currently working in that **29.**_____ get to see something from you by watching the show.

This further explains the fact that why some candidates who do not win but eventually are more successful than those who do. Let's not forget that ultimately it is those **30.**_____ who purchase the record, **31.**_____ or advertised products not those judges. Perhaps you have that quirkiness in you that you do not know it yet. That does not have to be **32.**_____ attractive....

A. Contrast to what we might have expected from the fashion assistant who has to be the stereotype by being stunningly beautiful, Betty Suarez is unique in her own way. That makes her get picked by Bradford Meade, the owner of the Meade Publications. Her coworker Marc St James is also a peculiar assistant, and the two might have been the best pick for their role as assistants. It goes to show that in addition to appearance, experience, and fashion sense, personal qualities are the key to get to the top or get the job down. Each possesses uniquely quirky traits that make them a suitable and loyal candidate for both their bosses, Slater and Daniel.

貝蒂‧蘇雷茲與我們對時尚助理所期盼的刻板印象有所不同，她並非有著驚豔的美貌，而是有著她個人獨特的風格在。那也是她被布拉福‧米德，米德出版股份公司的持有人所挑中的原因。她的同事馬克‧聖詹姆仕也同樣是位獨特的助理，他們倆位均是最佳的助理人選，且在職位上發揮所長。這也彰顯出了一點，除了外表、經驗和時尚觀感，個人特質是能否爬到頂端或是完成工作的關鍵所在。兩者均具備了獨一無二的奇特特質，讓他們成為斯萊特和丹尼爾兩位老闆的合適和忠誠的人選。

B. One of the daunting tasks given to Betty to see if she truly has what it takes to be Slater's successor is getting the crown. It was also the task once given to Slater by her scary boss, Fey Sommer. Getting the crown is not as easy as it sounds, and Slater had to use numerous scheming to get it.

其中一項交付給貝蒂令人心生畏懼的任務，以檢視她是否真的具備能成為斯萊特的繼承人是取得王冠。這也是一項曾由菲・桑默，斯萊特那可怕的老闆所交付的任務。取得王冠並沒有聽起來那樣輕而易舉，而斯萊特必須使用許多計謀以完成任務。

C. This happens right after Betty has helped Slater land a major advertiser during the meeting. Slater has listed multiple things for Betty to accomplish, and one of them is the tiara that Catherine the Great wore at her wedding to Peter III. Betty views this as a punishment for her conduct at the meeting, but in fact it is a test to see if she is qualified for the job. She successfully accomplishes all tasks, including lending the tiara, and that makes her outshine another assistant Marc. Marc jokes about her way of getting the tiara by listening to the curator's whining and crying. By being nice to someone is the key to lend the tiara. One does not necessarily have to do the nasty things to get the job done. The deal for getting the tiara also includes a full-page ad in the next month's issue. An ad space in exchange for using the tiara for 48 hours. Slater later says that "my methods were a little less wholesome than yours." and "there's been only one other person who's been able to get that tiara." Accomplishing a seemingly impossible task has proved that Betty has rare potential. One cannot argue that it's not her quirkiness.

這件事情發生於會議期間，貝蒂幫助斯萊特贏得一位主要的廣告商的贊助。斯萊特已經列出了許多項目要貝蒂去完成，其中一項就是取得凱薩琳女王在她與彼得三世婚禮中所披戴的王冠。貝蒂把這項任務視為是懲罰她在會議中的表現，但實際上卻是個考驗檢視她是否具備這項工作的資格。她成功地完成了所有任務，包含了借到王冠，這讓她表現得比另一位助理馬克更為優秀。馬克嘲笑她取得王冠的方式居然是傾聽館長發牢騷和哭泣。藉由體察他人卻是租借到王冠的關鍵。一個人並不需要做許多齷齪的事情才能完成交付的工作。獲得王冠的交易還包含了允諾在下期的雜誌中要有整頁的廣告介紹。廣告空間換取能使用王冠 48 小時。斯萊特之後提到，「比起妳的辦法，我當初使用的方法較沒那麼有益於人」。而且「一直以來，僅有一個人能夠拿到那頂王冠」。完成近乎不可能的任務證明出貝蒂具有罕見的潛能。一個人無法爭論那並非是因為她的古怪而使她辦成。

D. Another incident relating to Betty's uniqueness is the tico berry shoot. Kimmie sabotages the shoot by saying "have fun doing a tico berry shoot with no tico berries." Then she throws all the berries into a large pond, leaving all people stunned. With Betty's two bosses, Slater and Daniel staring at her, Betty tries to think outside the box, and she is the one who saves the day.

另一個關於貝蒂獨特性的事件是媞口莓果的拍攝。媞米破壞拍攝並說道「拍攝得開心點，沒有媞口莓果的媞口莓果拍攝」。然後，她就將所有的莓果丟進一個大水池裡，此舉讓所有人都驚訝萬分。貝蒂的兩位上司斯萊特和丹尼爾都盯著她看，貝蒂試圖跳脫框架想出辦法，最終也是她救了這次的莓果拍攝。

E. From Betty's life at Mode, how one person can be successful can be illuminated. In *America's Next Top Model*, during the deliberation of a particular episode, Tyra Bank, the host of the show, was asked about the same question as to how success of most winners of the show cannot last, and it was even before the publication of the bestseller, *Quirky*. There must be something, she explained, such as quirkiness, that makes them special.

貝蒂在 Mode 的生活能充份闡釋出一個人如何邁向成功。在《名模生死鬥》，特定一集的評審審議期間，泰拉·班克絲，該節目的主持人就被問到一個同樣的問題，就是在節目中勝出的大多數贏家，他們的成功都無法持久下去，而此回答甚至是在暢銷書《奇才》出版之前。一定有些因素，她解釋道，例如古怪性格，讓他們很特別。

F. The answer is quite meaningful and insightful, and we must not forget the fact that all judges have their preferences that create a bias against those who are truly great. Sometimes those judges have to pick the person who suits the image for the cover girl and the magazine that they have been working with in that particular season.

這個答案相當具有意義和洞察力，而我們不能忘記的是，所有的評審都有他們的偏好，因此對那些實際表現很棒的人的評估產生了偏差。有時候那些評審必須要挑選符合 cover girl 的形象的參加者，以及符合在某個特定賽季中所合作的雜誌。

G. For those who have participated the reality show, you simply cannot take the winning too seriously. It is great that if you eventually win the prize, but if you don't win and keep doing what you love and you will eventually find another way. You probably do not win, but that doesn't mean that you are not great. It probably conveys the message that your picture and style do not suit the company's ideal. There are other companies that are a great match for you. Not to mention, you have the exposure from attending the show, and multiple people who are currently working in that industry get to see something from you by watching the show.

對於那些參加過實境秀的參賽者，你不能把勝出看得太重。如果你最終能勝出的話很棒，但是如果你沒有勝出仍持續從事你所喜愛的事物的話，你還是會找到自己那條路的。你可能沒有勝出這項比賽，但是那並不意謂著你的表現不出色。這僅能傳達出一項訊息，那就是你的照片和風格並沒有符合該公司的理想。一定還有其他公司跟你會很合拍。更別說，藉由參加這項比賽，你有了曝光的機會了，而且很多現在正在這個產業工作的人也正觀看著比賽，或許他們之中有人就從你參賽後看出了你的亮點。

H. This further explains the fact that why some candidates who do not win but eventually are more successful than those who do. Let's not forget that ultimately it is those fans who purchase the record, magazine or advertised products not those judges.

Perhaps you have that quirkiness in you that you do not know it yet. That does not have to be physically attractive. Follow your heart and eventually will embark on a journey that amazes people around you.

這也進一步解釋了為什麼有些候選人沒有勝出，但是最終卻比那些勝出的人更為成功。我們也別忘了，最終是那些粉絲購買唱片、雜誌或是廣告商品，而非那些評審們。或許你身上就具備了古怪的特質，只是你尚未發掘到而已。那也並不代表說，該特質要是外表亮眼吸引人。照著你心中的想法走吧！最終會開啟一趟旅程，讓周遭的人都感到驚艷。

參考答案

Test 4
Reading passage 1 (1-13)

1. C
2. A
3. B
4. F
5. D
6. M
7. B
8. I
9. G
10. F
11. bombshell
12. appearances
13. aging

Reading passage 2 (14-27)

14. E
15. D
16. J
17. A
18. I
19. C
20. L
21. E
22. K
23. N
24. F
25. D
26. B
27. H

Reading passage 3 (28-40)

28. vi
29. ii
30. ix
31. v
32. x
33. vii
34. viii
35. successor
36. curator
37. more
38. two
39. exposure
40. judges

Test 4 P1

1. millionaire
2. assume
3. bombshell
4. outer
5. reluctant
6. determining
7. diploma
8. knockout
9. stagnated
10. agenda
11. struggling
12. innuendos
13. realities
14. unpleasant
15. preference
16. wealthy
17. outmaneuvers
18. inadvertently
19. skillfully
20. trivial
21. zeros
22. election
23. manipulation
24. clinch
25. castle
26. veto
27. divorce
28. settlement
29. pre-nuptial
30. stock
31. deed
32. tangible

Test 4 P2

1. resemblance
2. treason
3. fugitive
4. lawsuit
5. testimonies
6. intermittently
7. acquittal
8. likeness
9. confined
10. imprisonment
11. rouleau
12. diagnosis
13. atrocious
14. secluded
15. captivity
16. Paris
17. incarceration
18. agitated
19. doctor
20. prospect
21. suppresses
22. scarfs
23. vile
24. aristocrats
25. imminent
26. beheaded
27. penalty
28. recognized
29. document
30. defendant
31. probative
32. definitive
33. adduced
34. countenances
35. dire
36. inexorable

Test 4 P3

1. fashion
2. stereotype
3. coworker
4. peculiar
5. qualities
6. quirky
7. candidate
8. daunting
9. successor
10. scheming
11. advertiser
12. punishment
13. accomplishes
14. curator's
15. nasty
16. issue
17. wholesome
18. impossible
19. sabotages
20. pond
21. illuminated
22. deliberation
23. winners
24. publication
25. insightful
26. preferences
27. reality
28. exposure
29. industry
30. fans
31. magazine
32. physically

閱讀文章	參考書籍／電影／影集	引述句
TEST 1 READING PASSAGE 1	*How Luck Happens*	"The whimsical decision to toss away half the resumes is the perfect example of random chance."
TEST 1 READING PASSAGE 1	*Getting There*	"I'm a big believer in creating your own opportunity if no one gives you one."
TEST 1 READING PASSAGE 1	*Desperate Housewives*	"I suppose that we create our own luck."
TEST 1 READING PASSAGE 1	*Desperate Housewives*	"we are just not as lucky as you are."
TEST 1 READING PASSAGE 2	*Wikipedia*	"In a 2011 leaked information, adipose fins are related to sense, such as touch and sound, and water pressure."
TEST 1 READING PASSAGE 3	*Treasure Island*	"All of us had an ample share of the treasure and used it wisely or foolishly, according to our natures."

TEST 1 READING PASSAGE 3	*Treasure Island*	"Captain Smollett is now retired from the sea. Gray not only saved his money, but being suddenly smit with the desire to rise, also studied his profession, and he is now mate and part owner of a fine-rigged ship, married besides, and the father of a family. As for Ben Gunn, he got a thousand pounds, which he spent or lost in three weeks, or to be more exact, in nineteen days."
TEST 1 READING PASSAGE 3	*Homeless to Billionaire*	"not being able to recognize your passion can be a problem for those stuck in jobs that they do not enjoy."
TEST 2 READING PASSAGE 1	*Getting There*	"Some shows end up being hits, but two out of three fail."
TEST 2 READING PASSAGE 1	*Getting There*	"We get pitched about five hundred television shows a year and only put four new ones on the air."

TEST 2 READING PASSAGE 1	*Suits*	"You are five minutes late. Is there a reason that I should let you in."
TEST 2 READING PASSAGE 1	*Suits*	"I'm just trying to ditch the cop. I don't care if you let me in or not."
TEST 2 READING PASSAGE 2	*Treasure Island*	"Out of the eight man who had fallen in the action, only three still breathed – that one of the pirates who had been shot at the loophole, Hunter, and Captain Smollett; and of these, the first two were as good as dead."
TEST 2 READING PASSAGE 2	*Treasure Island*	"There is a kind of fate in this."
TEST 2 READING PASSAGE 2	*Treasure Island*	"You found out the plot, you found Ben Gunn – the best deed that ever you did, or will do though you live to ninety."
TEST 2 READING PASSAGE 3	*unknown*	"Life does not always give us the joys we want."

TEST 2 READING PASSAGE 3	*Getting There*	"anytime you experience traumatic loss early on it changes who you are and drastically affects your view of the world."
TEST 2 READING PASSAGE 3	*Way of the Peaceful Warrior*	"Who knows whether it is bad luck or good luck."
TEST 2 READING PASSAGE 3	*Way of the Peaceful Warrior*	"everything has a purpose, Danny; it's for you to make the use of it."
TEST 2 READING PASSAGE 3	*Ugly Betty*	"How can a girl get so lucky?"
TEST 3 READING PASSAGE 1	*unknown*	"Three heads are better than one."
TEST 3 READING PASSAGE 2	*Jane Austen*	"preserve yourself from a first love, you need not fear a second."
TEST 3 READING PASSAGE 2	*Gone with the Wind*	"Have you been running after a man who's not in love with you, when you could have any of the bucks in the County?"

TEST 3 READING PASSAGE 2	*Gone with the Wind*	"Our people and the Wilkes are different."
TEST 3 READING PASSAGE 2	*Gone with the Wind*	"He never really existed at all, except in my imagination."
TEST 3 READING PASSAGE 2	*Wuthering Heights*	"so that's enough for you? Just by being handsome and pleasant to be with, Linton can be your husband."
TEST 3 READING PASSAGE 2	*Wuthering Heights*	"he won't always be handsome, and young, and may not be always rich."
TEST 3 READING PASSAGE 2	*Wuthering Heights*	"all seems smooth and easy, where is the obstacle?"
TEST 3 READING PASSAGE 3	*Game players*	"We have created the most difficult so far."
TEST 4 READING PASSAGE 1	*Match Point*	"It's taken mother a while to get used to the idea that I'm serious about her. Mother's always had this funny little agenda for me which doesn't involve marrying a struggling actress."

TEST 4 READING PASSAGE 1	*Match Point*	"It's a particular cruel business for a woman and as you get older and time passes if nothing happens it gets harder and harder. But I am a great one for facing up to realities."
TEST 4 READING PASSAGE 3	*Ugly Betty*	"My methods were a little less wholesome than yours."
TEST 4 READING PASSAGE 3	*Ugly Betty*	"there's been only one other person who's been able to get that tiara."
TEST 4 READING PASSAGE 3	*Ugly Betty*	"have fun doing a tico berry shoot with no tico berries."
TEST 4 READING PASSAGE 3	Tyra Bank	"There must be something, she explained, such as quirkiness, that makes them special."

《八方旅人》

tremendously 極大地;極端地	**upend** 顛倒,顛覆
proficiency 精通;熟練	**preconceived** 先入為主的
daunt 嚇倒;使氣餒	**limelight** 眾人注目的中心
tentacle 觸手,觸角	**replenish** 把……裝滿,補充
regenerate 重建;再生	**pre-empt** 先發制人
transmutation 變形;變質	**apprehend** 逮捕;捕獲
resistant 抵抗的	**cachet** 封印;特徵
guard 保衛;守衛	**immobilize** 使…陷入癱瘓
impenetrable 無法穿透的	**exportation** 輸出;出口
shield 盾;保護	**auxiliary** 輔助的;附屬的
ineffective 不起作用的,無效果的	**dumbfounded** 目瞪口呆的
appendage 附屬物,附屬肢體	**seizure** 捉住;奪取
regrow 重生	**stationary** 停滯的
stagger 蹣跚而行	**shackle** 桎梏,束縛
hamstring 使殘廢	**erudition** 博學;學識
abdicate 放棄	**reconstruction** 重建,再建
intention 意圖,目的	**stature** 身高,身材
defeat 戰勝,擊敗	**replenishment** 補充;充滿

《雙城記》

trial 審問，審判	**miserably** 痛苦地；艱苦地
resemblance 相似	**secluded** 與世隔絕的
endure 忍耐，忍受	**captivity** 囚禁；被俘
treason 叛國罪，通敵罪	**entrust** 信託，委託
aristocratic 貴族的	**incarceration** 監禁
fugitive 逃亡者；逃犯	**departure** 離開；出發
lapse 陷入	**agitated** 激動的
lawsuit 訴訟	**prospect** 前景，前途
testimony 證詞，證言	**suppress** 抑制，忍住
intermittently 間歇地	**vile** 卑鄙的，可恥的
acquittal 宣告無罪，無罪開釋	**obliterate** 消滅；忘掉
statement 陳述，說明	**imminent** 逼近的；即將發生的
likeness 相像，相似	**penalty** 處罰；刑罰
attentive 留意的；殷勤的	**recognize** 認出，識別
imprisonment 監禁；關押	**incarceration** 監禁
resistance 抵抗，反抗	**defendant** 被告
rouleau （用紙包的）一捲硬幣	**probative** 供作證明或證據的
atrocious 兇暴的；殘酷的	**definitive** 決定性的；最後的

國家圖書館出版品預行編目(CIP)資料

雅思閱讀聖經 / 韋爾著-- 初版. -- 新北市：
倍斯特出版事業有限公司, 2022.01 面；
公分. --（考用英語系列；36）
ISBN 978-626-95434-1-0(平裝)
1.國際英語語文測試系統 2.考試指南

805.189   110021219

考用英語系列 036

雅思閱讀聖經（英式發音 附QR code音檔）

初　　版	2022年1月
定　　價	新台幣550元

作　　者	陳韋佑
出　　版	倍斯特出版事業有限公司
發 行 人	周瑞德
電　　話	886-2-8245-6905
傳　　真	886-2-2245-6398
地　　址	23558 新北市中和區立業路83巷7號4樓
E - m a i l	best.books.service@gmail.com
官　　網	www.bestbookstw.com
總 編 輯	齊心瑀
特約編輯	郭玥慧
封面構成	高鍾琪
內頁構成	菩薩蠻數位文化有限公司
印　　製	大亞彩色印刷製版股份有限公司

港澳地區總經銷	泛華發行代理有限公司	
地　　址	香港新界將軍澳工業邨駿昌街7號2樓	
電　　話	852-2798-2323	
傳　　真	852-3181-3973	